Night in the Metropolis
and Other Stories

Surendra Mohanty's

Night in the Metropolis
and Other Stories

Translated by

Gurudev Meher

BLACK EAGLE BOOKS
Dublin, USA | Bhubaneswar, India

Black Eagle Books
USA address:
7464 Wisdom Lane
Dublin, OH 43016

India address:
E/312, Trident Galaxy, Kalinga Nagar,
Bhubaneswar-751003, Odisha, India

E-mail: info@blackeaglebooks.org
Website: www.blackeaglebooks.org

First International Edition Published by
Black Eagle Books, 2023

NIGHT IN THE METROPOLIS AND OTHER STORIES
by **Surendra Mohanty**

Translated by **Gurudev Meher**

Cover & Interior Design: Ezy's Publication

ISBN- 978-1-64560-443-3 (Paperback)
Library of Congress Control Number: 2023945551

Printed in the United States of America

Contents

Translator's Note 7

Night in the Metropolis 19
The Gulmohar 31
The Wearied Emissary 37
Sacrifice 45
Discovery of India 53
Australia 63
Undefeated 70
First Rain of the Monsoon 78
The Editor 85
Ward No. 17 93
The Dying Dinosaur 100
Cigarette 113
The Guest 121
Bread and Moon 129
The Female Dancer 138
The Ruins 150
Adima and Shatarupa 173

Translator's Note

Surendra Mohanty was a versatile genius – journalist, freedom fighter, politician and litterateur. But his distinction lies chiefly as a litterateur. And even here his versatility manifests itself as a novelist, a short story writer, a literary critic, a historian and a biographer, though he is most prominent as a novelist and a short story writer.

Mohanty's concern is with the world of ideas, ideas born not from abstraction, but from experience and facts. Critics have traced the influence of Sigmund Freud in some of his writings. Mohanty himself states that some of his writings are influenced by James Joyce's stream-of-consciousness technique. In his substitution of extraordinary heroes for ordinary people in many of his writings and his vigilant role as a writer against neo-colonialists in a post-independent nation, Mohanty anticipates the ideas of postcolonial writers, especially Ngugi Wa Thiongo and Frantz Fanon. However, his writings are not confined to any theoretical framework. The presentation of the ancient and the modern, the rich and the poor, the elite and the illiterate, the spiritual and the mundane and the amalgamation of myth, history and contemporaneity impart universality, authenticity and relevance to his theme. Mohanty's style is marked by loftiness, sonority and grandeur which are the hallmarks of his craftsmanship. His style is characterised by embellishments. He quite often speaks in a different dialect and idiom from other writers. All these lend some kind of imperviousness to the translation of his writings.

He received Central Sahitya Academy Award and the Sarala Award for his novel and biography, *Nilashaila* and *Kulabruddha* respectively.

His other well-known novels comprise *Andha Diganta* (*The Dark Horizon*), *Niladri Vijaya* (*Triumphant Return to Niladri*), *Kalantara* (*The Changeover*), *Ajibakara Attahasya* (*Ajibaka's Satiric Laughter*) and so on. Ruti o Chandra (The Bread and the Moon) Mahanagarira Ratri (Night in the Metropolis), Maralara Mrutyu *(Death of a* Swan), Mahanirvana *(The* Salvation). Yaduvamsa (The Yaduvamsa), Krushnachuda *(The* Gulmohur) etc. are some of his famous short stories.

The theme of his novels ranges from the innocence of village life to the futility and complexity of city life, from the helplessness of human beings to the sublimity and grandeur of human life, from the romantic exotification of the past to the relentless commitment to a nation's history and cultural heritage, from the corrosion of political values to the wonderful presentment of mythical stories, and from the miraculous dramatization of life's ordinariness to the justification of the eventless drama of life. His uniqueness of theme, treatment and presentation provides him with a special place in the history of Odia literature.

Surendra Mohanty, through his literary crafts-manship, has revolutionized Odia short stories written in the post-independent era by introducing new trends and techniques to the existing narrative. He deliberately seeks to present his characters in a largely absurd and irrational world which is rather suggested as a derivative of the inner fragmentation and rupture they inevitability experience living in a disorderly, chaotic world. Mohanty made his stories appear startlingly lifelike through his deft manipulation of the linear narration, his reluctance to judge the characters, his judicious, hyperactive attention to detail, and above all, his disinclination to achieve final climactic moments in his short stories. Most of his finest stories are open-ended and without a clear narrative resolution which necessarily points out the developing sense of incompleteness and disintegration that has informed modern life in general.

Each of his stories, therefore, serves as an emphatic onslaught against the rigidified bound of experience and strives to champion the cause of the unprivileged and the marginalized. His stories are poignantly graphic and often leave the audience with an overriding feeling of emptiness. He seems to eternally suspend his characters between the conflicting sense of defeat and triumph, desire and fruition, power and helplessness. He is the first to introduce symbolism in Odia short stories which helps him to subtly allude to the meaning of something without being overtly expressive. His descriptions of the outward, invigorating nature necessarily correlate with human feelings and instincts and turn out to be indispensable tools for exploring the mysteries of the inner landscape of the mind.

Mohanty's style is characterized by loftiness and sonority, grandeur and pomposity. He is sometimes charged with employing inflated language in his novels and short stories, but this grandiloquence rather stems from the profundity of thought and terseness of expression with which he deals with the complex emotions and feelings and the manner he continues to explore dignity and grandeur in the eventless drama of human life.

In his fictional maneuvers, it is difficult to differentiate between the world of the physical universe and the world of ideas which are somehow intermixed, and to exalt the one is to exalt the other for his ideas do not merely originate from dry speculation, but from experiences and facts. It is, however, impossible to place the author in a particular class or group as he deals with a variety of different concepts and themes that fascinate his thinking mind. His impressionist presentment of scenes does not seek to impose moral judgement on the reader irrespective of the occasional authorial comments and remarks that are scattered in his short stories. It is worthwhile to mention that Mohanty is always at his creative best in his short stories than in any other genre because nowhere was he so successful in sustaining the dignity and grandeur throughout, both in terms of form and content, than in the limited space of a short story.

Night in the Metropolis and Other Stories is a collection of seventeen short stories by Surendra Mohanty and is very popular among the readers of Odia literature. The stories incorporated in this collection were written in the formative period of his artistic career and unmistakably bear a tinge of his early romanticism which is allied with an ever-questioning spirit of understanding the universe. The writer is particularly sensitive to the contemporary conflicts, contradictions, struggles and socio-cultural problems of the world he sees around him. In this collection, he has artistically presented the hopes and aspirations, the idealism and the humanity, the optimism and the worldliness of a bunch of blundering individuals, living in an imperfect and confined ambience of city life. But the inherent connection of city life with village life is nurtured beautifully till the end. The writer has used his writing as a mission to champion the rights of the oppressed and the marginalized. The protagonists in his stories are generally centralized around some defining qualities. They nourish a liberal outlook towards life and are humanistic, free, undefeated, and sharply individualistic. The evil environment fails to affect their outstanding personalities. They carry out their perpetual struggles against adverse circumstances amidst thousands of injustices, oppressions, treacheries, penury and disgrace. Mohanty feels that literature should address the problems of human life and society. Not simply the problems that concern the question of livelihood but the ones that necessarily relate to the spiritual and emotional aspects of human life.

The short stories in this collection project a familiar world that is created out of the writer's lived experiences in which the characters are evaluated through different specific moral standpoints against a troublesome world of heterogeneous inclinations and affiliations. Each of his stories, therefore, is a product of his intense self-analysis and introspection. They are the outcome of his emotional distress and serve as a means to alleviate his concealed sense of anguish. Writing is thus put to therapeutic use that is re-creative of the inner poetry of the private self and which is evoked by emotion and not by dry speculation.

The title story "Night in the Metropolis" depicts the life of a disgraced prostitute named Chandra, living in a dingy flat in the sophisticated setting of Calcutta city. The story narrates the reality and the prevention that inform her character as she develops a fresh relationship with the gentleman she welcomes to her flat in the advanced hours of the night. The story finally proves that pretense is as painful as the experienced reality. The stained character of Chandra is contrasted with the innocence and effervescence of her younger sister Minu who was still a virgin but "would soon lose her virginity to some lustful man that she had respectably preserved for years. And then, the voluptuous sybarites of the metropolis would feast on her delicate flesh. But when this flesh would exhaust its resources, it would again be thrown away into a dirty ditch like some left-over chicken bones by the roadside."

The writer condemns the pimpish civilization which seeks to negotiate the urge between the flesh of an unfortunate woman and the carnal desire of a lustful man, equating the job of a pimp with that of a politician, a lawyer and a saint, and regrets that these men would someday sell off the soul of the country to some affluent trader. They are not going to suffer any loss as they must get their share or percentage.

The subject of the story, "The Wearied Emissary" is based on an unforgettable episode of Hebrew history. The narrative begins with a beautiful description of the gigantic pyramids that stand splendidly on the sandy planes of Egypt and a series of rhetorical questions that begin to plague the mind of Hebrew Moses. It delicately dramatizes a significant portion of ancient history in which the old exiled Moses led the Jews out of slavery in Egypt and ushered them to the Holy Land that God had promised them. Here Mohanty, with the help of an obsolete historic persona, has bridged the gulf between history and contemporaneity that serves as a wake-up call for the slumbering humanity.

The story titled "Sacrifice" is set in a remote Santal village surrounded by towering sal forests that nourish no connection with the outer world. It tells the romantic story of Binodia and Mahua backdropped against the freedom struggle of Jharkhand which was subsequently made a separate state of India. The tranquility of the village life is suddenly disrupted when some men from Patna reached the village and led the innocent tribal into a bloody struggle with the armed forces of the Odisha Government. The story ends with the sad demise of the protagonists when the writer asserts: "Many evenings had passed after the incident, but the showers of gulmohar were no longer greeted by the cascading *kuruchi* blooms. Nobody had also got the news as to how many Binodias had been racked with anguish by the pangs of Mahua's painful departure."

The story "Discovery of India" graphically presents the man and manners of the post-independent Indian societies. Pandit Jawaharlal Nehru wrote his book *The Discovery of India* in 1945 but he failed to present a true picture of India which Mohanty has sought to compensate in this story. Veering us away from the richness and prosperity enjoyed by a particular section of society, it focuses on the ordinary, uneventful life of the commoners who feel alienated by the elegance and refinement of urban life. It further regrets the loss of a glorious, magnificent past and the way it was made to follow a downward trajectory.

"The Editor" is a powerful satire on the corrupt political leaders and power mongers of our country who have now replaced the patriotic, nationalistic and dedicated leaders of pre-independent India. The so-called able leaders of the state lacked the conviction and fire to lead a nation and the incompetent people are full of passionate intensity to lead the mass through blood and tears. The story argues against the myth that our world will get peace when the love of power will be replaced by the power of love.

The eternal conflict between wealth and talent is the central theme of the story "Undefeated." Saroj was a salaried officer. Mrunmay was a millionaire and the editor of the *Messenger*. But despite his being highly talented, Shyamal was forced to live a life of penury because he failed to strike a compromise between wealth and talent. Saroj said, "Talent has lost the battle against wealth for long, Shyamal, and this defeat is not personal that has influenced my life, but it has occurred worldwide. Talent has become a slave to wealth and property!"

The sentiments expressed in "The Editor" are reflected in the problematic concerns of the story "Undefeated" to which the writer responded in the story "The Guest." The story-teller here seeks to redefine the ideals of leadership in India as the protagonist finally returned to the village as a guest which he visited before and was suddenly invaded by the love and affection showered upon him by the poor villagers.

"The Dying Dinosaur" narrates the life and time of the despotic Brajeshwar who refuses to strike a compromise with the changing time. His character is portrayed as an enormous unsatisfied soul that perpetually longs for the lost magnificence and grandeur of monarchy. He is perhaps the only character in this collection of short stories who genuinely detests affecting artificiality in his demeanour and does not hesitate to pass acid comments on the drawbacks of democracy. Thus, when the tiny beauty spot under Sundari's lips is accidentally smudged by her hand, drawing a black line across her chin, he exclaimed,

"There was absolutely no necessity of painting a rose with hues." It is one of the finest stories of Mohanty in which a former king mourns the abolition of the monarchy and finds himself as a rare specimen like the extinct dinosaur.

The story titled, "The Female Dancer" is an artistic outpouring of Surendra Mohanty's romantic propensities. Backdropped against the construction of Lingaraja Temple by Yayati Keshari, it admirably depicts the tragic tale of Devadasi Purnima and the young sculptor Natawar and the tender love that blossoms between them. Natawar seeks to immortalize Purnima after her death with the stone-carved life-like figure which he sculpted on the inner wall of the Lingaraja Temple with great diligence. The story presents the eternal conflict between the head and the heart, God and the human, the physical world and the imaginary heaven. It works as a crude satire on the obsessed mankind who has turned a blind eye to the beauty and charm of human existence in their relentless pursuit of religion, temperance and divinity.

"Bread and Moon" is based on the perpetual conflict between the need to earn one›s daily bread and the desperate craving for the coolness of the moonlit night that ails the common humanity in all ages and climes. The mighty walls of communism seem to crumble before the beauty and charm of human life which cannot simply be reduced to a formula of production and distribution. The story finally explores the fact that the established tenets of communism, which has rendered the bread more attractive than the moon, ultimately fail to grasp the real problems that concern mankind. It provides a constructive critique of the Marxist philosophy by exposing its lack of concern about human feelings and sentiments and its overindulgence in the centralizing economic indicators as the only determinants of common welfare.

The leadership of Binod, the local communist leader, was really commendable in organizing the masses and inspiring a revolt against the exploitative capitalists. Lalita used to praise Binod›s integrity and his erudition on Marxist philosophy. When Binod was busy with his party bulletin, Lalita›s curious mind began to be fascinated by the beauty and charm of the moonlit night. Looking wearily at the framed photograph of Marx, hanging on the wall of the party office, Lalita was given to musing as to whether the bread was more fascinating than the glowing moon. Is sustenance the only aim of human life on earth? She enquired from Binod if Marx had said anything about the moonlight night anywhere. The story is structured around a corresponding antithesis between the real and the imaginary. Reality is highly desirable, but the delight and charm of living cannot be experienced by running endlessly after reality. Mohanty, in his presentment of this inner conflict, rather focuses on the mental dereliction and spiritual sterility of his characters which prevents them from realizing the worth and significance of natural beauty. As Lalita powerfully observes: ". . . many struggles and revolutions had gone futile and become extinct in the process of arguments and altercations. Yet, this fine moonlit evening seemed eternally graceful. There was no end to its conduction of delight."

The story titled, "The Ruins" beautifully depicts the history of an aristocratic family that covers five generations of the Chaudhury clan. It begins with Nataraj Chaudhury who is a clever and efficient man. After gaining the support and favour of the Britishers, holding high offices, he can lay the foundations of the Chaudhury Estate. The story moves through the lives and times of the descendants such as Vishwapati, Umapati, Nilamani and finally Rajendra during whose time the eventful history of the Chaudhury family has almost become a legend. It appears as if the worn-out, emaciated skeleton of the Chaudhury family is lying neglected in the graveyard of unending time. Rajendra is so passionate about the complete obliteration of the past and nourishes the dream of absolute demolition in his mind. But he is inwardly optimistic that one day the majestic Chaudhury Palace will be restored to its former glory.

The characters of Adima and Shatarupa have been drawn after Adam and Eve described in the Genesis of *The Bible* as the first man and woman of the Creation. This story titled "Adima and Shatarupa" dramatizes with psychological details the fall of mankind as a result of the eating of the forbidden fruit. The story, however, emphasizes the creative impulses of Adam and Eve amid their blossoming love relationship and final union. Man represents power and strength and woman beauty. Creation is only possible by the fusion of beauty and power. Thus, they are finally united after many aborted advances on their parts: "Ah, what a wild, horripilating excitement was that! How painful yet how pleasing! And what mad craving to lose oneself in the equivalent other!"

Night in the Metropolis and Other Stories is above all an artistic outpouring of Surendra Mohanty's socio-cultural fervour and is an appropriate vehicle of his broad human vision and ardent revolutionary zeal.

The readership for this book includes scholars and researchers across the globe and a large section of people from India and abroad who are not native speakers of the Odia language. Only a very few of Surendra Mohanty's works have been translated into English to date. It is because of the apparent imperviousness of his language which is highly ornate, formal and stylized. This explains the reason his works are hardly rendered into English despite his being the most acclaimed writer of post-independent Odia literature. Therefore, I feel this book to be widely read and appreciated by people of India and abroad.

Gurudev Meher

Night in the Metropolis

The restless scream of a steamer in Ganga Jetty sounded in the distance.

The desolate street of Chaurangi looked phantasmal like the abode of the dead in the serene light of the low-lighting electric lamps.

Chaurangi—a mecca for the trading culture.

On the other side of the tram road, refugees, in groups, slept on the bare soil. The metropolis seemed stark and bereft with a dusty surface below and a midnight sky overhead. Bidis and cigarettes were still glowing at random every now and then. The blazing fire in the furnaces was flickering by either side of the street.

The solitary moon of the bright fortnight swayed seductively as it sauntered along the highway of heaven. The British Dance Club in the vicinity had long since been closed. Gentlemen, clad in foreign apparel, were coming out from the club, at regular intervals of five or ten minutes, whistling their favourite numbers.

Chaurangi Pavement.

'Salaam Sahib!'

'Salaam!'

'Do you want a girl?'

'Nonsense!' I yelled out at the man. 'What are you saying?'

But it was his daily business. The man became apprehensive for a moment and then said, 'Not too far from here, sir. It's just down Park Street Lane.'

I stepped forward. My entire body shuddered with disgust and embarrassment. Oh, how I wished I could shoot the man dead like a dog! How mean! How despicable! But he was just one of the representative figures of this pimpish civilisation. Acting as an intermediary between the individual and the state when one earns the respect of a political leader, acting as a middleman between the jurisprudence and the client when one gets the prestige of a lawyer, and acting as an agent between God and man when one can assume the status of a saint, then why should it be deemed dishonourable to act as a pimp, negotiating the urge between the flesh of an unfortunate woman and the lewd longing of a lascivious man. Strange is this pimpish civilisation and its trading culture! These individuals may eventually peddle the soul of their nation to a wealthy merchant. They won't experience any losses since they're guaranteed to receive their fair share.

Perhaps a man hid himself behind the shadow of a pole by the street. As I approached the place, he suddenly pounced and stood before me like a predator on its prey.

The same promo repeated: 'Not too far from here, Babu, just at the turning near Park Street.'

I turned, looked behind, and saw the first man getting inside a taxi with a jaded sybarite, dressed in foreign apparel. I moved ahead keeping my distance from the man as if I heard nothing. The man walked a few paces following me and then went back. A coachman was hailing cheerfully at some tourists as he pulled his horse-drawn carriage along the lonely street, 'Come on Saab, Badabazar! Badabazar Saab!'

Another man yet again. And the same words continued to be repeated: 'Just down Park Street Lane!' I looked at his face for a moment. The man began to describe the turning near Park Street at length.

'Is it how you earn your living?' I inquired.

'Yes, Babu,' said the man rather disinterestedly. 'A handsome sum of money from percentage and tips.'

And then, the tempting promos of Park Street Lane continued to attract potential customers.

*

But it was not at the turning near Park Street, rather a long way ahead of it.

It was a starry night in March. The climate was hot and humid, and a mist of warm steam was rising from the hot surface of the earth. The persevering earth was sighing deep and long with heart-rending exasperation. The silk-cotton tree on the right of the road was clad in numberless red flowers. Numerous families, including husband and wife, brother and sister, father and mother, son and daughter had now drifted into slumber in those pigeonhole-like tall buildings.

There was an alley behind the row of tall buildings, and a narrow winding sub-alley, leading to a flat on the ground floor. Sounds of drunken revelry and loads of uncontrolled laughs were issuing into the night from those dingy flats on the upper floor. Gosh, was this Park Street Lane?

The man called out and knocked lightly at the door with the iron chain. The door was flung open. The lady who opened the door perhaps was the enchantress of this Park Street

Lane. I cast my gaze downward in shame and embarrassment. I even did not know what I was thinking at that time looking downward. Slightly shoving me up, the man said, 'Tip, Babu!' I groped in my pocket and handed him a five-rupee note. He thankfully accepted the sum and greeted me with his usual expression, 'Salaam!' Then he looked up at the lady of Park Street Lane, and demanded, 'Sister, my share please!'

'What else,' I asked.

'My percentage,' the man pleaded.

I handed him another five-rupee note and said, 'You may leave now.'

The man walked away whistling a merry tune. The lady of Park Street Lane gasped at my face in stupefied amazement and said, 'Please, come in!'

My throat was feeling incredibly parched with a raging thirst. I entered the room and said, 'Can you give me something to drink?'

'Of course!' said the lady and called someone by her name. 'Minu, Minu!'

After a few minutes, a young girl of about thirteen or fourteen years hurried into the room, rubbing away the sleep from her eyes. There was mild irritation in her face but it rather had multiplied the beauty of her blooming lotus-flower-like face by leaps and bound. The lady promptly instructed the girl to bring a bottle of beer and some blocks of ice.

I felt relieved to find that the lady was fashionable having good taste. Minu went away. Her long lethargic braid, like the animated arm of a lustful man, was girdling around her fleshy hips as she walked engagingly into the room. A beautiful red rose adorned her black braid. But it seemed almost fondled to death, looking pale and lustreless.

I was fixedly looking at her with rapt attention.

'She is my sister, Babu,' said the lady. 'Still a virgin.'

Maybe the lady assumed I would insist on Minu's young flesh. But has this flesh ever quenched this body's raging thirst? No, it's just for your mind. She should have been treated with respect as a daughter rather than eagerly relished as a mistress.

Minu returned with a tray laden with a glass of beer with ice in it and placed it on the table.

'But you didn't fetch the cigarettes,' said the lady.

Minu was going to fetch some cigarettes for me when I said, 'I have got them with me, thanks. You may sit here.'

Minu sank into a nearby chair. Her eyes were laden with excessive sleepiness. I was suddenly invaded by an inordinate desire to gently place her head on my lap and lull her back into a restful slumber, telling stories about the prince and the princess from some fanciful fairy tales. The prince was mounted on a fabulous horse that was said to swiftly carry its rider to the desired place. The princess was seated on the prince's lap, his arms softly wrapped around her slender waist. The horse was racing with the speed of an arrow. And an unsightly, horrible giant, returning to his cave, was chasing after them with a vengeance.

'I'm leaving, Didi,' said Minu, lazily stretching forth her sleepy limbs. 'The ache in my head has worsened.'

Minu lifted herself from the chair.

Her long braid waved elegantly over her enormous, spherical hips. But she left behind a conglomerated fusion of sundry incompatible emotions such as compassion, sympathy, fondness, hatred, inclination, and filial affection.

I peered at the lady's face after Minu left. She must be about forty years of age. Her skin had grown wrinkled with time. Her advanced age had already creased some crooked lines around the corners of her otherwise beautiful eyes. Yet she had shown no parsimony and spent lavishly in grooming herself as a young lady in her twenties. Her face was covered with layers of pale-coloured foundation and white paint used for makeup. She put on red lipstick on her lips and wore patches of rouge on her cheeks. Despite these, she seemed to be quite older than she was. If she had a son, maybe he would be my age now.

But God knows, how we two happened to be together in this dingy flat on Park Street Lane. I heard the clatter of two empty beer bottles under the sofa. The ashtray on a nearby table was crammed full of cigarette butts.

How dreadful was this incarnation of woman! The daughter, the wife, and the mother who once thrived under this wrinkled skin were ruthlessly crushed to death by this grim reality of subsistence and what was fostered was but an unrelenting, gruesome hunger, cloaked in the image of a woman. Its hunger had not yet been satisfied even after devouring the soul of the man. How ghastly and appalling it seemed! My fur bristled up in horror and disgust.

Everyone's face carries some common marks which remind us of yet another face. Similarly, the two semicircular lines forming around the lady's mouth, reaching from the nostrils to the chin, reminded me of one lady I met some years back.

I was travelling from Howrah in Delhi-Panjab Mail. The interclass compartment was so thickly crowded that it was impossible even to add a mustard seed to it. I journeyed from Howrah to Asansol in a standing position as no seat was vacant. At one corner of the long berth, a Hindustani lady was seated, spreading a blanket on it. On seeing me she said, 'How long will you keep standing, my son? Please, be seated here!'

I huddled up into one corner of the berth avoiding eye contact with the lady. The lady tried to dispel my fear, asking me to sit comfortably, 'There is nothing to feel embarrassed, Babu. You are my son's age. My son is also staying in Delhi. I am going to pay a visit to him.'

In the face of that lady also two semicircular lines were running from the nostrils down to a point in her chin. But those lines seemed smooth and delicately creased across her face, unlike the one I noticed here on the face of this lady which was furrowed in deep crinkles. This lady too, upon meeting me somewhere in the street, must have greeted me enthusiastically by calling me a son. But here, at this moment of the midnight, down this Park Street Lane, she was seated before me, wearing patches of rouge on her cheeks, and having applied a thick dusting of translucent powder all over her wrinkled face!

The silence was getting unbearable with each passing second. It would be a great relief to escape from this place.

'What's your name,' I asked.

'Chandra,' she responded, and said in a familiar voice, 'Please, come in. How long will you keep sitting there?'

I handed two cash notes to Chandra and said, 'The night is getting denser, let me leave now.'

Perhaps Chandra was musing inwardly that she had no moral right over this unexpected sum of money. She was about to say something when I opened the door and said, 'Kindly give half of it to Minu.'

'But, she's still a virgin,' I heard her saying behind my back as I walked away.

The moonlit night of the March became instantly intoxicated. Minu would soon lose her virginity to some lustful man which she had respectably preserved for years. And then, the voluptuous sybarites of the metropolis would feast on her flesh. Again, when this flesh would exhaust its resources, it would be thrown away into a dirty ditch like some left-over chicken bones by the roadside.

*

It was twelve o'clock the next night. I was again on Chaurangi Pavement, confronting the same question of the last night: 'Do you want a girl, Saab?'

I was walking towards that flat on Park Street Lane.

The door was locked from the inside. I jingled the door chain. The door swung open. Minati, alias Minu escorted me inside the room. I went inside and sat on the same sofa I was offered to sit the last night. Minati's blooming lotus face was glowing with delight and freshness and looked more elegant than before.

'There are two men inside,' said Minati. 'Didi is coming very shortly. You may sit here and relax.'

'Oh, I see.'

'Let me fetch a beer for you.'

'No, thanks. Only a glass of water, please!'

Minati returned after a few minutes and put a glass of water on the teapoy. She was about to leave when I said, 'Please be seated, Minu.'

Minu curled up hesitantly in one safe corner of the sofa feeling insecure.

'Where are you from, Minu?' I asked.

Her eyes became moist at the query, with drops of tears rolling down her pronounced cleavage.

'But what makes you cry?'

'We hail from a place that is far away from here, Babu. We had to run away from our home. My father went missing. My brother was brutally murdered. Finally, my mother . . .'

Minu could not say anything more. The unhappy, luckless mother was ultimately forced to sell her daughter down Park Street Lane to relieve the burden of her life, weighing upon her feeble shoulders.

Today, the world is so awash in the ingredients for sobbing that it has become very common for people to cry uncontrollably at the slightest provocation. Through this process, the world's tears may have totally dried up. So, while feeling immense sympathy for her misery, I was unable to shed even a single tear.

'Are you able to read and write, Minu?'

'Yes, I can read books.'

I pulled out a small book of fairy tales from my pocket and gave it to her, 'Keep it with you, Minu. Do read this when you suffer from mental anguish.'

Overcome with a youthful caprice of her mind, Minu swept her fingers across the glossy front cover of the book. An extraordinary picture of an unknown prince adorned the front cover of the book. Mounted on the fabulous horse that was said to swiftly carry its rider to the desired place, the prince was gliding effortlessly through the open firmament to rescue his prized princess, held captive in some dark dungeon in a remote wonderland.

Perhaps Minu was reflecting on the possibility of such a happy rescue by the prince of her dream. Nay, possibly he would not be able to come. The magic wings of the fabulous horse had been broken in the middle of the thick forest on the outskirts of the slumbering metropolis.

The noise of the chaotic steps of Chandra and her two inebriated sybarites sounded as they descended the broad staircase. Minati lifted herself and went away.

The two men left the room. Chandra flung the door shut and sat closer to me. I could smell the awful stench of cheap gin emanating from her body. I pulled myself back in disgust.

'Not here today, Babu,' said Chandra with a smiling face. 'You must come upstairs.'

I did not like it. Yet, invaded by an insatiable curiosity, I acceded my consent to the proposal and followed her upstairs. There was a luxuriant room on the upper floor meant for love-making and drunken revelry. The whole floor was littered with empty whisky and soda bottles and stomped cigarette butts.

Chandra carelessly perched on a nearby sofa. She was struggling with certain dizziness resulting from the gin and whisky intoxication.

Suddenly, I came across a framed photograph placed at one corner of the dressing table. It was the photograph of a young man having bright eyes. I approached the dressing table and began to examine the photograph. Chandra conducted herself hurriedly from the sofa, snatched the photograph from my hand, and put it back inside the drawer.

'You needn't panic, Chandra!' I promptly said. 'There is no harm to have a close look at the photograph of your stunning lover.'

'You want to know who he is!' Chandra returned in

a quivering voice with tears running down her bright face as she began to weep bitterly. 'He is my son, Babu, whom I have carried in my womb for months together. And he is not an illegitimate child. Alas, they stabbed him to death before my very eyes! I witnessed on that day how a man was reduced to a savage beast driven by wild instincts and vicious inclinations. They killed my husband in the same manner. They only left me unharmed just for my body which they enjoyed with great relish. I somehow escaped from their evil clutches and came to this place.'

She buried her face in my bosom and wiped bitter tears at her misfortune like an abandoned, unsatisfied child. Unable to withstand the stench of gin, I wanted to shove her off my body with all my strength. Yet I miserably failed. Ah! I like you to weep your sorrows away, Chandra, if your oppressed soul may be restored to peace by crying!

After some time, Chandra lifted her head from my bosom and silently sat on the sofa. The paints applied over her face were washed away by her rolling tears, exposing the swarthy, pale skin underneath that looked ugly, hideous like corroded metal. The beads of tears in her inebriated eyes were shining like two metallic fire bulbs.

I groped in my pocket and handed two cash notes to Chandra and said, 'I'm leaving, Chandra.'

'No, Babu, I won't let you go today, the two drunkards . . . ' Chandra could not complete her speech.

It was five-to-two in the midnight.

'No, Chandra!' said I. 'I must leave now.'

Pressing her lipstick-coated lips against my face, Chandra screamed, 'No, no, you can't go, Babu, leaving me alone!'

I felt as though somebody had forcibly stuck a piece of burning charcoal on my body. I slapped her in the face that was smudged with make-up paint, and sternly said, 'Release your arms, please.'

'Babu!' Chandra cried out in a wounded voice with an air of puzzled bewilderment.

'Do not call me Babu,' I said angrily. 'Call me 'my son' instead. Had your son been alive . . . '

'Oh, God!' Chandra buried her head against my chest, weeping big, hot tears.

The night of the metropolis greeted her words with derision.

Her voice reverberated, floating amid the restless scream of the steamer, gliding past the shore along Ganga Jetty.

The Gulmohar

The office of the weekly newspaper *Sangram*.

Sadanand was reading the proof. It was a damned old building. Water leaked through the damaged roof whenever it rained. Rainwater continued to stream along the floor. One side of the inner wall was covered with a thin layer of moss.

The unrestrained downpour of the early monsoon had now thinned out to a faint drizzle. Crippled with weariness and dejection, Sadanand pushed aside the proof sheets to one corner of the table. Reading proofs for years together, he had turned unnaturally into a bitter cynic. He was only confronted with errors and mistakes wherever he went.

There were still four pages or 16 columns left for proofreading. The pages of the newspaper were yet to be filled with those 16 columns before printing. With a grimace of annoyance, he pulled a cigarette from his pocket and lit it.

He was everything in the office—the editor and the proofreader at the same time. There was of course another staff in the office but he would only handle the external affairs.

Sadanand aimlessly walked back, opened the window and peeped outside. For a long time, he had not gotten a single opportunity to stare at the outside world like this.

A gulmohar tree stood adjacent to the window. The green top of the tree was concealed completely beneath the gulmohar's brilliant blossoms.

How beautiful! Nay, it was saying too little to call it simply beautiful. It was rather a flamboyant expression of the gulmohar's beauty, softness and youthful exuberance.

The dark, fecund clouds in the overcast sky were dying to touch the sodden earth as much as the gulmohar ardently lounged in the lap of the thickening mist. It appeared as if the swarthy head of a pious Vaishnavite was adorned majestically with a bunch of red, bright flowers freshly plucked from the garden of heaven above.

The cigarette was finished. Sadanand threw the burning butt through the window.

There were still 16 columns left!

Blind with fury, Sadanand slammed the window shut. In this old, slavish world, life had been reduced to a futile, meaningless existence. A world comprising of docile and obedient slaves! Slavishness has sucked the zest for life from the marrow of every inhabitant living on this planet Earth.

Then what precisely is the difference between Sadanand and a coolie from the suburb down the street? The coolie is a slave to the owner of a factory and Sadanand to a particular ideal or idealism in general.

There's even a sense of fulfilment in the coolie's simple, unadorned life. On receiving his wage at the weekend, he will drink a few bottles of cheap country liquor with great relish and continues to live a life of absolute contentment. But Sadanand did not have that well-earned little luxury either. A brooding sense of discontent and anxiety had enveloped him from the beginning of his life to the end. His cherished ideals reached no fulfilment.

A blast of cold wind blew open the windows.

The beautiful colour and brilliance of the gulmohar that was now matured with freshness and vigour was a mockery of the moribund existence of a slave like Sadanand. A whoop of derision!

Meanwhile, many years had passed. One day Sadanand had decorated Tamasha's chignon with bunches of bright red blooms of the gulmohar flower in his own hands. It was a long time ago when Tamasha first stepped into his house as a new bride. Perhaps that was also a lazy afternoon like this pouring with rain in the month of Ashadha.

Today, of course, his ageing hands had lost most of their former spirit and liveliness.

There were still 16 columns left!

Sadanand returned to his table. But what would he fill those 16 columns with? Britain's brokerage? Russia's rising communism? America's index of affluence? India's intellectual sterility? Sadanand had little patience left to fill his columns with such stuff.

Well, could not one write an article on the gulmohar tree in the newspaper? This wavering, elegantly graceful gulmohar in its flaming scarlet glory which had replenished the mild, silent afternoon with life and motion?

Nay, the gulmohar was an irrelevant creation in the editor's universe. The whole world would deride its portrayal in a newspaper column.

But is it impossible to imagine a polity where the meaning of life is much more than just earning one's living? A world where the ultimate goal of life is not the acquisition of an empire or achieving one's supremacy over others? Not consolidation of power or exploitation of others in the name of growth and development? But a world where there is also a place for the gulmohar as well.

Sadanand came back again and sat near the bunch of proof sheets.

But today it seemed as if his mind revolted against that constricted corner of the office room. The swaying gulmohar had raised that saffron flag of revolt in the world outside.

Sadanand hypnotically lifted himself from the chair and hurried out of the room.

It had stopped raining. Sadanand came and stood under the gulmohar tree. There were multitudes of red petals scattered over the bed of grass under the tree.

The blooming passion of youth began to pulse through his veins. He desired to climb up the tree and pluck as many flowers as he wished.

But inwardly Sadanand could not gather enough courage to do so. What the world would say if he climbed on a tree at this age and plucked gulmohar flowers? The whole world would ridicule him for his eccentricity. He looked in all directions. There were humans everywhere, wherever the eye glanced. Countless humans—ugly, abominable, biped animals!

Here Ramesh is coming down the street. Now he must have come across some difficulties to complain about.

'Oh, you are loitering here closing the office!' Exclaimed Ramesh. 'How would the compositors get their wages tomorrow?'

'I don't know.'

'What do you mean?'

'Please leave me alone, Ramesh. Do not vex me any more.'

Ramesh went away completely bewildered.

After a few minutes, Sadanand returned to the office. There were humans everywhere. He had no courage left to climb up the tree and pluck the gulmohar flowers.

It was a late hour of the night.

The waning moon of the dark fortnight rose calmly in the cloudy vault of the night sky.

A streak of faint moonlight, streaming through the open window, illuminated slumbering Tamasha.

Sadanand had no sleep in his eyes. His eyes were glittering with the merry dreams of the dancing gulmohar flowers.

Was it that Tamasha on whose chignon he had once tucked clusters of colourful gulmohar? No, this was not that Tamasha, who first came to his house as a new bride, on whose neat bun had been accumulated the charming illusion of the dwindling night enshrouded in the thick gloom. Now that Tamasha was dead and gone.

When a man dies, his soul dies with him without his conscious knowledge. For the rest of his life, he is compelled to live the uneventful, inglorious life of a mere slave.

Tamasha had died, and so had Sadanand.

Sadanand dragged himself from his bed and furtively went outside. The same gulmohar tree stood invitingly before him in its full glory and splendour beggaring belief.

It appeared as if the swinging branches of the gallant gulmohar laden with bunches of reddish blooms were fanning the slumbering earth with a massive chowrie.

Sadanand stood under the gulmohar tree. He was preparing to climb up the tree when he suddenly felt his limbs had turned inert and powerless. His body had lost its former strength and vigour. He drastically failed to sustain the agility and youthfulness of his heart and spirit.

Still, Sadanand began climbing the tree applying all his strength and might.

'Who's it?' came a voice from behind, startling Sadanand.

The constable on night duty. Wrapped in a raincoat from head to toe. He had a cudgel in his hand and a smouldering bidi dangling in the corner of his lips.

Sadanand got down from the tree.

A beaming torch light showered upon him illuminating his startled face.

'Oh, it's you, sir! At this late night hour?'

Confounded, Sadanand blurted out, 'Oh, no, it's nothing!'

Sadanand came back from there with quickened steps before the constable spoke anything more.

The earth was dead. And so was Sadanand. The glamorous gulmohar stood there majestically as a dolorous memento of a magnificent past brimming with vibrancy and energy.

The Wearied Emissary

2 000 BCE …

The flat and featureless desert of Egypt.

Vast rolling dunes and arid deserts filled the Egyptian planes. Pyramid after pyramid stood splendidly on the desert sands constructed by the pharaohs like the dumb, feather-brain scholar of relentless history. The pages of history remained unfilled, its significance perpetually eluding his loosening grasp. The pyramid stood there in hopeless silence, gaping at the pacific firmament, expecting to finish his writing of a strange, ruthless and oppressive history.

An old man, clad in thick white fleece, appeared behind a dune and stood near the pyramid. He was faint with hunger, his face covered in an elongated grey beard that reached all the way down his waist. The dense overgrowth of grey hair on his head was creating the illusion of a snow-capped forest. He held a staff in his hand.

The fugitive Hebrew Moses!

Tell me O pyramid, the wisest and astute one; thou hast witnessed the waxing and waning of many a civilisations and empires' fortune, blest with vision and far-sightedness as thou, why is man filled with such callous disregard for other fellow humans? In this pious world of Jehovah, everybody is born with an equal right to live. Yet, how is it possible that a man for the sake of his personal profit never minds depriving others of that similar right to live? Why does this injustice prevail over this beautiful world? What does this lack of fairness proffer? Tell me, pyramid, why is this world plagued with such grave injustices?

A maelstrom of emotions crossed the old man's wrinkled face, with tears rolling down from his sunken eyes.

Nay pyramid, thou canst never furnish an answer to this oppressive question! Thou art at the disposal of the pharaohs, founded upon the timid blood of innumerable Hebrew slaves. How do thee grasp human suffering?

The old man walked away, dragging his weary feet through the desert sands. Everywhere, he was surrounded by vast, sprawling dunes, meeting the dim horizon of the sky. There was no end to his relentless journey.

The sky began to explode as the blood-red sun sank below the western horizon behind the Sinai hills on the coast of the Red Sea.

A bloody war was waged between the massive clouds in the western sky. The western sky seemed to drown in the ocean of blood. The gigantic, grave Sinai hill was visible against the backdrop of the blood-red firmament. The old man looked behind and heaved a long sigh. Then, leaning on his staff for support, he slowly ascended the hill. There was a lonely cave at the peak of the hill. The old man dwelled inside it.

The dawn was about to break, but sleep continued to elude the old man's eyes. In one corner of the cave was a burning candle made from sheep's fat. In that faint light of the candle, the old man was busy writing the cursed history of a nomadic nation on a piece of rock, holding a sharp rod in his hand in the Sumerian alphabet. His pale eyes, at times, glowed like molten fire bulbs against the darkness of the cave. Like the drippings of wax from the burning candle, a solitary tear trickled down his pale cheek. A sudden gust of cold wind howled about the empty cave and made the old man shiver. The glowing flame of the candle flickered merrily against the backdrop of the night, casting eerie shadows over the untidy surface. The old man placed the iron stylus on the floor and dejectedly fixed his gaze on the dancing flame.

It was the beauteous expanse of the Ur Mountain range. The Euphrates flowed meanderingly from one of these mountains towards the fertile, lush and green valley of Babylon. One day, the entire Ur reverberated with the anguished wails of lakhs of starving nomads. Acute scarcity of food and drink plagued the whole land and crops failed due to extreme weather conditions such as low rainfall, drought and heatwaves. Wherever the eye moved, it was only greeted by rocks, boulder stones, hills and rough mountains. Not even a single blade of grass was visible in the entire expanse. The ravenous hunger of the nomads had exhausted all edibles of the land without a trace. But they were in dire need of food, fertile soil and bountiful harvests.

The next day, before the dawn broke, lakhs of poor nomads, in groups, defying the dread of the impenetrable darkness, began to trudge along the rough path of the Ur Mountain range in the quest for fertile soil and independent life. It was a sort of pilgrimage for these homeless destitute.

Look, there . . . nope, it cannot be achieved so easily! Where? How far? Is it within the range of your view? Not yet! But the water of the Euphrates is as clear and pure as the cloudless sky, the soil as soft as Jehovah's divine blessings and the landscapes as evergreen as the benign affection of a loving mother! Babylon—the ultimate shrine of this prolonged pilgrimage!

The day broke, darkness fell and it was repeated again and again. Yet, there was no end to this arduous journey.

The ultimate pilgrimage of life!

No, no, do not look back, move forward. Do not wait for those that lagged. You must keep on walking, rampaging over the fallen multitudes. You must walk interminably to reach your object of pilgrimage, albeit it looks like a distant dream.

They nourished hunger, desire and fierceness in one of their eyes and dreams, ideals and serenity in the other. Yet, Babylon eluded their restless vision.

See, Babylon, there! Where is it? Where? Is it visible from this point? Ay, one can see the ruins of the Sumerian civilisation, the domes of Babel! But where are the Sumerians? And where is that topless tower of Babel which stands for their Promethean pride? Ask for it from the Akkadian whose hunger for power exhausted the pride of the mighty Sumerian. Alas, the fate of the Sumerian civilisation! But where is that invincible Akkadian either? Ask the Amorites whose power struggles similarly dissipated all pride, strength, confidence and valour of the Akkadian. And lo and behold, the top of the majestic palace of Hammurabi, the King of the Amorites. Again, the Amorites were subject to the insatiable hunger of the Hittites.

This hunger for power is real, eternal and has eclipsed the whole universe like a dark shadow.

Lakhs of starving nomads angrily roared out in agonising gnawing hunger.

These golden wheat fields, the neighbouring vineyards, and the blue Euphrates, however, were a wonder to behold.

But, no sooner had they stepped on the frontier of

Babylon, the Babylonian army launched a series of onslaughts on the famishing nomads. Babylon along with the green valley of the Euphrates had learnt from past experiences as to how deadly would be the outcome of this insatiable hunger that had engrossed the entire world. Let that hunger be systematically murdered in cold blood!

There was no way to go back where but reigned perpetual hunger, agony and death. There was no strength left either to move forward; the path looked endless like a boundless ocean of sprawling sands.

Where should they go then? Ah, Jehovah! Ah, Hebrew! Alas, poor nomads! The awe-inspiring sight of Egypt began to greet their weary eyes. The beautiful, glorious Nile flowing through this land was a feast for the eyes, its water fathomless, salubrious and life-giving. A nice, shaded place, overhung by date palm trees! There were beauty and charm in life!

The journey finally ended in Egypt. Of course, Egypt sheltered these refugees. Unlike others, it did not object to their living in Egyptian society. Because it required thousands of naive slaves to build numerous gigantic pyramids for its pharaohs. The Egyptians needed them to break and carry loads of solid rocks from the impassable mountain range situated on the northern sides of the Nile.

Suddenly, a gust of wind rocked the dying flame and the only source of light flickered away. A lurid luminance was visible at the opening of the cave as the dawn broke in the eastern horizon, but there was no end to the old man's brooding rumination. The sound of some footsteps was audible outside the cave.

'Is it Solomon?' the old man queried.

'Yes, we have come,' a voice responded from outside. 'Who else?'

'Isis!'

Two men, wearing grey fleeces, entered the cave.

'I was waiting for you for long,' said the old man.

Then abruptly, all of them fell silent for a few moments. As if words stopped at their lips, unsounded. The lurid luminance of the dawn was gradually fading into a crimson light outside the cave.

'Are you ready for the inevitable?' asked the old man. 'I have received Jehovah's bidding that at this crucial point, we must begin our ultimate battle. And this time it is Palestine, our beloved motherland—the ultimate pilgrimage! Our fate is unshakably tied to that holy place to which we naturally belong, where we shall get enough fertile soil to grow our green harvest and our servile souls will be happily delivered to a new human world.'

'But the armies of the Pharaohs are firmly posted to stop our progress at each step,' said Solomon. 'They are concerned as to who would carry the lofty rocks for them after we depart from this land.'

'Slavery is not the aim and objective of human life on this Earth, Solomon,' the old man roared. 'A life of liberty is better than mere existence and I have heard that call of freedom from heaven.'

'Well, issue your order,' said Isis, 'and do tell us when we are supposed to begin that cherished struggle for freedom? If needed, we are prepared to combat the armies of the Pharaohs.'

'Today, tomorrow, day after tomorrow . . . any day you can prepare yourself for the final battle,' said the old man. 'I am ever prepared for it.'

'Tomorrow,' Solomon blurted out.

'Yes, tomorrow,' Isis added.

The Canaanites in Palestine soon came across the news that lakhs of hungry nomads, the slaves of Pharaohs, were rushing towards Palestine from the West in the quest for freedom, soil, and food. They would occupy Palestine by force which they hailed as their beloved motherland, the ultimate destination of their life.

The fierce Canaanite army marched forward like deadly eagles to launch a violent attack on the Hebrews. The desolate valley of Palestine reverberated with the sounds of military gongs and kettledrums.

Moses remained fearless and unperturbed. 'Now, you must pay the price of your freedom,' he declared, leaning on his staff for support and addressing the terrified nomads. 'Behold, this craggy mountain range. Here you can see sacred Palestine, the object of your relentless quest, penetrating the pale horizon of the deep sky. That is our holy shrine, our ultimate pilgrimage, the destination of our prolonged journey. Look there and you can see the fierce Canaanite army marching forward to collect the price of freedom from us. Remember, in this beautiful world of Jehovah, everybody has an equal right to live, including ourselves.'

'We're ready to pay that invaluable price of freedom at any cost,' lakhs of hungry voices cried out in unison. 'But we need fertile soil, an abundance of food and unfettered life!'

Lakhs of mighty muscles instantly became animated with wild excitements. Moses sat down on the sands overcome by extreme fatigue and weariness of the long and arduous journey.

A bloody battle ensued between the Canaanites and the Hebrews. The Canaanite army could not withstand the Hebrew assault and like a feeble sandbank soon merged away in the meandering current of the Hebrew onslaught.

The old Moses stood up again and began to exhort the victorious Hebrew, 'Do not bewail the loss of the dear ones and try not to defile this golden moment of triumph by shedding warm tears. Those who died in this battle have paid the price of freedom for us. Do salute them with utmost reverence. They proved themselves as the martyrs of this freedom struggle whose worthy blood has cooled this impassable desert path to liberty. Do bow your heads before them, whose bones and flesh have levelled and filled the cracks of this rugged pathway. They have emerged as the loving sons of Jehovah. Let their souls be ushered into heaven!'

Moses' nimble feet had suddenly become inert and lifeless. There was no strength left to move forward. His will to live might have exhausted itself after the attainment of that prized gift.

His powerless body tumbled down the warm sand. His weary eyes glowed with the unfamiliar dream of tomorrow.

'No, no, you must march ahead without looking behind, trampling my worthless body under your triumphant feet. But make yourself noble, gracious, kind-hearted and free. O Jehovah, damn tired as am I, do grant me respite now!'

The old man's eyes began to close as with the blissful sleep of death by degrees.

Palestine was just a few steps away.

Sacrifice

It was a Santal village in the Saraikela province. On each side, the village was surrounded by towering *sal* forests. Since a time in the ancient past, life continued to flourish along this shaded Santal village in the most uneventful and ordinary manner. It had no history of its own. Nobody in the world was curious about the general life in the village. Neither were they bothered about who was devoured by the tiger at twilight in the *sal* forest or who was hanged on the charge of murder or who had gone to war and never returned home. They were but trifling events of day-to-day life. Daylight would break in the eastern sky; the sun would rise above the mountain and also drown in the ocean of *sal* forests. As darkness fell, the pucca house in the middle of the village would be flooded with country liquor, produced from *mahua* flowers, and with that meandering current, the nimble feet of the young men and women would become animated with the hypnotic rhythm of the music and folk dance.

Nobody in this Santal village had ever imagined that there existed an enormous world beyond these sky-high walls of the *sal* forests. The village had no connection with the outside world. Every year, on the day of the Chaitra Festival, the men and the women of the village would flock to the King's Palace in Saraikala. They would again return to their village in the evening, and the desolate, untrodden path of the forest would reverberate with the festive frolics of songs and music.

It was their life and their world which was intimately their own. Looking through the glasses of experience, they even found the soil more deeply rooted in their respective lives.

But those who were comparatively new to this tiny world rather discovered it to be bigger than the former one. And this new world had become enlivened in their imagination which was even more welcoming to them. It was Jharkhand. The contours of this territory, however, are yet to be chalked out by their sensible minds. The Jharkhand of their dream only existed in their wilful imagination. They had heard about this Jharkhand in Ranchi from their political leaders. In that prized land, there was no penury, no exploitation, no sorrow, and where eternal spring reigned the entire year. Traversing the long distance by foot, they went to Ranchi, lifting the burden of a bunch of wood on their heads, and carrying a fistful of flattened rice in the folds of their dirty clothes as their only belongings. After their return from Ranchi, the peaceful Santal village again resonated with the sounds, let out in the praise of their beloved Jharkhand, 'We shall take hold of Jharkhand by struggle. We shall take hold of Jharkhand by slaughter! How shall we take hold of Jharkhand?'

The young women of the village would respond by saying:

We shall take hold of Jharkhand by shooting arrows,

We shall take hold of Jharkhand by endless slaughter!

*

Only a few days were left for Chaitra Festival. The pleasing fragrance of the *mahua* flowers was permeating the cool air of the village. The *sal* trees were ablaze with brilliant red blossoms. The branches and foliage of the silk-cotton tree were ceremoniously clad in colourful flowers of the spring. The flowers in the gulmohar tree outnumbered its tiny leaves. The sumptuous effervescence of the flowering spring had also delved deep into the pulses of the young Santal women.

It was a time in the evening.

The young men and women were enjoying themselves in the pucca house, merrily dancing to the captivating rhythm of the music. The old men of the village were seated relaxedly around the blaze of a burning log to overcome the weariness of the day's labour.

The young men and women swayed elegantly to the tune, celebrating the festive exuberance of their intoxicating youthfulness. The song composed by the Vaishnavite Santal poet, Devananda sent ripples of agony amongst the young Santal girls as they burst into singing the song of life in unison:

The night rolled in the sportive forest

The cuckoo sings as the dawn breaks,

I waited long hours with my garland of flowers

Yet, Mohana still eludes my love-drunk eyes.

O my friend, the cruel Mohana has not come yet,

And the very thought agonies my barren breast

Thus, speaketh Devananda . . .

Life is doomed with endless delays.

The song continued to resonate with the pulsating rhythm of the music. Mahua plucked some *kuruchi* blooms from her curl and threw them onto Binodia walking amidst the menfolk. The young men carried bunches of gulmohar flowers in their tuck-in folds. *kuruchi* blooms from the womenfolk were generously greeted by the gulmohar flowers from the men's side. The darkness of the evening quivered in excitement with the beating of the tambour and the accompanying flute tune.

Right at that moment, some tribal men, who had come to this village from some distant place, hurried into the pucca house. They were from Patna, the capital city of Bihar, and had been sent out by the political leaders of Jharkhand. All songs and dances instantly stopped after their arrival.

The visitors had no time to relax. The Government of Odisha was snatching their territories from their hands. The Odisha police had already captured Saraikela and Kharsawan. Now, the villagers could not afford to indulge in song and dance any longer. They must get united and fight against the police force of the Odisha Government. All people irrespective of youth and age had to join the uprising. The visitors were sent off with this bidding. They had no time to waste.

The peaceful sky of the evening was resounded with the slogans, sung in the praise of Jharkhand.

We shall take hold of Jharkhand by struggle!

We shall take hold of Jharkhand by shooting arrows!

We shall take hold of Jharkhand by endless slaughter!

*

Before dawn broke, thousands of tribal began to crowd the mango orchard at the extremity of Kharsawan Garh. They held bows and arrows on their shoulders and battle axes in their hands. They continued to march in long meandering lines like armies of ants. The entire mango orchard was pulsating with the mad shouting of the people, fighting for Jharkhand: 'We shall take hold of Jharkhand by struggle!'

But what was Jharkhand? Nobody among the crowd was aware of it. And those few who knew about it were hundreds of miles away either in Ranchi, Delhi, or some safe corner of Bihar.

The crowd of the armed tribal was growing in number with each passing hour. How wild and uncivilised they seemed! Yet how innocent they were! They looked even more naive and ignorant than an innocent child. Because they thought they could withstand the power of the Bren gun and the Sten gun of the Odisha police force with their handmade weapons of bows and arrows prepared from bamboo.

After midday, a large procession of the tribal people meandered towards the palace of the garh. Before them stood the armed forces of the Odisha Government with their Bren guns and Sten guns.

It was, however, not a new thing to happen that day. An old chapter of human history was going to be repeated on that gloomy evening yet again. A group of few men, for the sake of the soil, had made thousands of our people addicted and crazy like this. And another group sought to invent new weapons of mass destruction to eliminate these mindless people. Nevertheless, it was branded as a noble act of patriotism by both groups.

The chanting of slogans by the crowd rose in a whirling crescendo, 'We shall take hold of Jharkhand by struggle!'

The procession was moving at a snail's pace.

At that time, another group of drunken tribals joined the throng from Jamshedpur's side. Like the raging of a storm, their inebriated throats blurted out in frenzy, 'We shall take hold of Jharkhand by slaughter!'

The tribals were gradually getting more violent with the spread of terror among them. Some of them shot arrows with their bows. The Odisha police began firing with Bren guns. The entire place became shrouded with the noise of the bullet and smoke. The tribals took to their feet and blindly fled to safety. Yet the Bren guns were firing incessantly at the fleeing tribals.

Binodia clasped Mahua's arm and ran for cover amidst the panicked dispersal. Oh, they might be saved hiding behind the trunk of a certain tree! The bullet shot by the police hit Binodia's right thigh and a stream of hot blood gushed forth from the wound. His body was getting inert and powerless by degrees. Men and women lay scattered around the ground like chopped-off trees and plants. Yet a few moments before, they happened to be the most vocal and active among the crowd . . . 'We shall take hold of Jharkhand by slaughter!'

Suddenly a bullet went straight through Mahua's back. She let out a huge scream and tumbled down to the ground. There was no time for Binodia to react. He collapsed on the ground behind a *sal* tree and lost consciousness.

*

It was a dark ominous night. Nobody was around. Screams and wails of pain prevailed in the entire place. Some motor trucks, beaming their large yellow lights, were moving around the fields. These trucks would soon be piled high with dead and half-dead bodies of the tribal people before vanishing into the darkness of the night.

After thousands of years from today, perhaps their bones would have been transformed into old fossils. Had any archaeologist ever happened to unearth those shuddering remains from some deep layers of the soil; he would throw them away as damn useless stuff. But if he would enable himself to read the history written on those worn-out fossils, he would be surprised to know how violent, inhuman, and uncivilised were mankind in the twentieth century. Exactly as we are perturbed at the human sacrifice performed as an offering to the deity in primitive societies. The committed atheists of the twentieth century had discovered a new god. And that god manifested in the form of mindless people or a country or a nation or in that special benediction insinuated by the political leaders of the state.

But it would happen thousands of years from today, not now. Yet this human sacrifice of today would serve as the first step to a promising heaven.

*

The editor of *The Searchlight* lifted himself from his chair and elatedly paced around the room for a few moments. For a quite long time, he had not received such sensational news items to fill the first page of his newspaper the headlines of which would sprawl four or five columns at a stretch.

Clinks of whisky glasses echoed in room no. 217 of Imperial Hotel in New Delhi as they raised their glasses for a worthy toast.

The ruler of Bihar in Patna Secretariat ran his tongue over his dry lips in pleasure and satisfaction. Cuttack Secretariat issued a communiqué expressing concerns over the whole incident... 'We are very sorry!'

And here, cries of distress, anguish, and curses billowed into the indifferent sky from the huts of the innocent tribals.

Many evenings passed after that incident. But the showers of gulmohar were no longer greeted by the cascading *kuruchi* blooms. Nobody had also got the news as to how many Binodias had been racked with anguish by the pangs of Mahua's painful departure.

*

After some days, the news was broadcasted: 'Saraikela and

Kharsawan were merged in Bihar. An official message was released from Ranchi: 'It is our Jharkhand!'

Chanting of slogans reverberated around the tribal villages surrounded by *sal* forests, 'Jharkhand Zindabad!'

*

The day after the event.

The ruler of Bihar was coming to Saraikela via Jharkhand. Flurrying their way through the dense overgrowth of woods and forests, thousands of tribal flocked to Saraikela. A large public ceremony was being organised in Saraikela. But the kinsfolk of those people, who had paid the price of this evening celebration with their lives, were plodding along the roads with weary steps like unbidden strangers.

Invaded by a thrilling sensation, they began shouting, 'Jharkhand Zindabad! We shall take hold of Jharkhand by struggle!'

The police constables of Bihar wielded their cudgels and yelled out at them, 'Say long live the ruler of Bihar!'

Discovery of India

The book *The Discovery of India* written by Jawaharlal has been released.

To the surprise of everyone, the book shot up the best-seller list.

To tell the truth, these groundnuts are scrappy. But this cone-shaped case, prepared from a scrap of paper, containing groundnuts, is wonderful indeed. All such old but strange news that has escaped your attention at first reading will again be cast before your eyes in the most unexpected ways when you desultorily sweep your eyes over them at some leisure hours. Oh, I see, Jawaharlal discovered India towards the end of 1945! Not bad actually.

One day, the bread vendor gave me a piece of bread enwrapped in an abandoned love letter. The bearded man Rashid Mia was an unromantic fellow. How insensitive he was to waste the beautiful love letter by wrapping it around a paltry bread!

What time is it now? 12 o'clock at midnight? Well, why do these groundnuts sell more in the evening? It is because people eat more groundnuts in the evening. But the groundnut vendors stop selling groundnuts after 9 p.m. And these groundnuts are cheaper than rice and a healthy diet too. It is, therefore, more beneficial for Indian people to eat groundnuts. Nope, I must have to write another book on the discovery of India as I see it!

Has Pandit Jawaharlal Nehru ever mentioned these things in his book? How many pieces of cigarettes one requires per day? You have to wait at least 8 hours before the cigarette stall opens. Nothing to worry about, my friend! Human life continues to run in this manner. Life is long, yet the resources you need to run your life are limited.

At least, after the end of the war, peace has been restored and this cigarette conjures up memories of those fond old days. The hopes and prayers of all the smokers of the world: Let the world be left in lasting peace. Oh, it's refreshing! But who is the discoverer of this thing called tobacco? Is it Walter Raleigh? Nadrek? Martin Luther? Whoever that may be, he must be one of the world's greatest men—worthy of his being!

Clad in a star-studded dark robe, the black, ancient sky seems gracefully reposed, with eyes laden with sleep. The beautiful, lofty, elegant sky of India! Has Nehru ever mentioned this calm, restful incarnation of the Indian sky in his *The Discovery of India*? Or should I write another book on the topic to recompense the lack?

The clock struck 1 at midnight. A slumbering hatchling from some dark corner of the nest, shrouded in leaves and foliage of the pine tree, awoke from its sleep with a jolt. Piercing the shadow, cast by the electric lamps, a flash of lustreless lightning illuminated the scruffy bedding that looked like a lustful young woman, desperately longing to unite with her lover. Nay, sweetheart, I'm not able to join you this night. My eyes have become swollen with the passion for discovering India.

The broad highway of the city has fallen fast asleep, seeming docile and expressionless. The yellow beams of the electric lamps by the road linger comfortingly on the hard surface. The mysterious highway of the dreaming night! Nobody can surmise where it ends at the threshold of some ceremonious portal in some magic land forlorn.

The story begins right back in the seventeenth century. Vasco da Gama's discovery of India! The socio-cultural life of India was torn amidst civil wars, internal conflicts, political stratagems, lavish emperors, and armed insurgents. Ah, that multicoloured robe of India that is woven from golden fabric fetched from the wonderland of colour and light!

Three centuries later, Jawaharlal again discovered a new India. The India of the emerging Hindustan and Pakistan! The India of the Indian National Congress with its deadly dagger of revolution, drawn on the shoulder of British imperialism!

Sky-kissing buildings stood on both sides of the road the heads of which were buried deep in the bosom of the darkened sky. Numberless lives had rested peacefully inside those tall buildings that treasured with care multitudes of people's hopes and aspirations.

It was a cold December night. The sharp, cold wind was pricking the skin like the sharp teeth of a wild animal. This old prehistoric overcoat under which I had passed many such winter nights now faltered drastically before the coldness of this wintry night. It, however, continued to give warmth and comfort when you put your hands in your pockets and turned your collars up against the chill.

This new, peculiar India seemed strange, dreadful and miserably inadequate. The resourceful India which once escaped the dreamy, radiant, unblinking gaze of the

Portuguese explorer Vasco da Gama, also eluded Jawaharlal's absolute, aggressive, nationalist outlook even after three centuries of mad struggle like the six curious blind men of India who strived to appraise an elephant by touching the different parts of its body. But what did they know about India?

A flame of fire was joylessly glowing by the edge of a drain along the roadside, casting long shadows across the surface. Surrounding the fire were seated some swarthy, skinny, human figures of the new India. Some of them covered their wrinkled skins with black refuse sacks. And others wore torn, abandoned coats, gathered back from some dirty dustbins.

'Cashmere Shawls Available Here'—the signboard was hanging on a nearby Marwari shop. It was brightly illuminated by the electric lights hanging on the poles by the roadside. The flame of fire, glowing by the drain, was getting dimmer and dimmer by degrees. Someone gathered a basketful of litter, scraps and dry vegetable skins from a nearby bin and poured it into the dying flame. The flame flared up again licking around the fire.

'It's one of the coldest winters as I feel. I won't go to pick up the passengers from Madras Mail any more.'

'Then lay sprawled on the fire.'

'Hahaha-hahaha-hahaha!'

Who were they scoffing at? The wintry night? Their destiny? The erroneous judgment of mankind? Or Panditji's discovery of India?

'O Allah, have mercy on me and grant me sustenance... grant me sustenance!'—A beggar, clad in torn clothes, appeared from some dark corner of the road, and sat near the fireplace. He was thankful to Allah for providing him warmth in the raging fury of the winter night, 'All praise to Allah, the merciful!'

Strange was this new India where Cashmere shawls helped people to beat the freezing cold of the evening and the broken basket and dry vegetable skins flared up, piercing the wombed darkness of the wintry night!

I was walking along a road of the city that ran winding through many lanes and turnings like the unsolved riddle of the advancing human civilisation amidst which humans had lost their easy movements and destinations. Setting out on that menacing maze of streets and alleyways, I embarked, my eyes laden with the dream of discovering India!

They were not skyscrapers in the true sense of the word. But you can harmlessly call them Indian skyscrapers. They were of medium height and built of reinforced cement concrete and were completely immune from the heat of the day, the coldness of the night, and the suffering and ordeal of the people living on the highway. One cannot help giving credit to this modern architecture that has wrapped an impenetrable drape around the shoulders of industrial capitalism.

Some destitute wayfarers crammed into one corner of the walls outside. To protect themselves from cold they curled up into tighter positions, hugging themselves like helpless, perplexed, powerless victims, ready to be hunted down by an accomplished hunter. But to tell the truth, human skin is not lacking in warmth. Has Jawaharlal discovered the fact that the Indian skin surpasses the Australian fleece, Canadian wool, and Cashmere shawls in giving warmth? I do not know.

It was an alleyway. The soft kerosene lamps lighted on both sides of the alleyway were gradually getting dimmer in want of fuel. The flickering flame down the roadside began to dance with an unknown excitement, as if.

I was walking through a red-light district—the breeding ground of gonorrhoea and syphilis germs. The gloomy brothels and whorehouses of the new India are modelled on the ideals of virtuous women like Sati and Sita! The doors of the houses on both sides of the road remained closed, open, or half-opened. Some swarthy figures had been sitting behind the doors, twiddling their thumbs and curiously waiting for some delayed sybarites to turn up.

The faint light of the street lamps illuminated their pallid, bloodless faces. Peering at their faces, one could notice the procession of gonorrhoea and syphilis germs, meandering through the blue veins under their wrinkled skins. They had been reduced to damn living shadows of their former selves. Their eyes were listlessly fixed on the vacant road in mute silence. The constable on the night shift was dozing on the veranda of the brewery, located in the middle of the street. Perching behind the mess of leaves and foliage, the nocturnal owl began its ominous, screeching hoots, piercing the deafening silence of the wintry night. In its ominous hoots was latent an emphatic query, 'O the explorer of India, have you ever discovered the breeding ground of gonorrhoea and syphilis germs?'

Have you ever explored when and in what circumstances these prostitutes living on their physical beauty came into existence? And at which evil hour this ultimate curse on human civilisation, this supreme disgrace to femininity called prostitution originated?

But I have discovered! The cigarette stuck between my lips glowed in delight at the cherished discovery. Yes, I have discovered! Do you want to hear where this swarm of degenerate women, looking like disposed broken teacups by the edges of the drain, came into existence? They have emerged out from the wombs of pious, upright women such as Sita and Savitri who are revered as the paragons of virtue and chastity!

Do you want to be clarified about the breeding ground of gonorrhoea and syphilis germs? They were bred at that cursed moment of the dawn when this capitalist, authoritative, acquisitive civilisation reconceptualised the ideals of virtue and chastity.

This social evil called prostitution began in that sinister moment of human history when the curtain of reason was draped on the pure and perpetual love between men and women. It had begun since that disquieting day when the primitive pulses of humanity were silenced under the sophisticated gravestone of ethics.

The clock struck five. Dawn would break in an instant. Yet, the roadway to the discovery of India sprawled endlessly before my restless eyes!

*

A desolate station platform.

Dawn broke and weak light filtered over the horizon behind the white clouds and thick fog. Standing on the platform, some TTEs, doing night duty, were slurping their tea in front of a tea stall. They were dressed in a warm overcoat, covering their bodies from head to toe. The railway engine in the distance was roaring loud sighs like a poor, abandoned destitute, bewailing his shadowy misfortune, being defeated against the prolonged battle of life.

An American soldier in uniform was pacing to and fro along the platform, waiting for some morning train to arrive.

Has Panditji written in his *The Discovery of India* about this lonely emigrant soldier who carried the delight of democracy in one eye and the dream of his beautiful, blue-eyed beloved across the seven seas in the other? Nay, Panditji has only discovered the heartless robots of imperialism, concealed in that unfeeling Tommy-gun-equipped soldier. But he fails to discover the tender heart beneath the thick uniform which is even more delicate and graceful than the lingering dewdrops on the blades of grass in the early morning. He has also not discovered the anguish and helplessness of this 'piece' on the chessboard of world politics.

Crossing the railroad, flocks of poor, homeless beggars, clad in disparate grabs and guises, were walking along the lonely street. Each of them held an empty, corroded metal bowl in their hands. Floating above the foreground of the bright eastern horizon, they sauntered around like nightmarish dreams of late midnight.

Has Panditji discovered this ancient, corroded, metal bowl of India where generous kings like Karna have sacrificed their life and their kingdom for the sake of truth? Has he ever given any clue as to when is this empty, corroded, metal bowl of India introduced to Indian society? Perhaps not. But I have discovered those vital facts!

'A cup of tea, please.'

Alas! This man's life would be wasted away pouring tea from the kettle for his entire life. What would he grasp of my discovery? Drawing out his hands, daubed with the stain of charcoal, from the oil-saturated pockets, he would now ask for his payment, 'Two annas, Saab!'

Gosh, is it tea or sherbet? Panditji must not have mentioned in his *The Discovery of India*, I swear, that the tea, sold in the Hindu stalls of the railway platform is even inferior to water in quality.

Have you heard about the history of this corroded beggar's bowl? It appeared in Indian society on that day when generous Karna's treasury had exhausted its resources in charity. These swarms of beggars also mushroomed over the entire country, splitting the arid soil of glorious India when the charitable Karna was born into Indian political history.

Giving alms in charity is but sheer bribery to protect the distressed conscience of the oppressor from an anticipated moral onslaught.

Motor trucks, loaded with paddy, were heading steadily towards the nearby rice mills, the sound of sirens blaring from the rice mills suddenly pierced the quiet ambience of the morning, signalling the beginning of the first shift. It was loud, sharp, and unpleasant. The Coolie Street in the distance reverberated with the noisy uproar of the day. Defying the coldness and the hunger of the morning, the coolies hurried along the path of the street like personified sin in search of their daily work. They looked as miserable as a sin and as terrible as a crime!

Looking up at the motor trucks, loaded with golden harvests, their stony, bedimmed eyes became animated for a moment with an unknown expectation and began to roll in their sunken sockets.

Has Panditji in his book *The Discovery of India* alluded to these meandering motor trucks, brimming in golden harvests and these forsaken sinners for whom hunger had proved a sin and penury a crime? No, he has not. His vision was not broad enough to penetrate through the towering walls of the Red Fort.

Like any other day, the customers began to crowd on the veranda of the tea shop on the Coolie Street. They slurped the hot tea from their tin mugs and chattered among themselves in blithe unconcern. Their shift of the day was yet to begin.

The new sun of India was rising above the horizon of the eastern sky.

Let the sun shine at its resplendent best in the glorious firmament. Long live the new dawn of India!

I finished my discovery of India. My eyes were bruised at the dolorous discovery.

'Hey man, pull your rickshaw,' I drawled.

Australia

My pocket was torn.

I fished up an uncurrent four-anna coin lying in one corner of the pocket.

In the affluent world of two hundred billion people, my only asset was merely an uncurrent four-anna coin!

But the owner of the tea shop was a nice man. He had already given me three cups of tea on credit since morning.

The cigarette vendor too was sympathetic towards his customers and did not insist on ready cash or quick payment of the unpaid amount.

It was a busy main road in the city. A stream of countless people was steadily meandering along the busy road. They hurried along this main road after the daybreak. Their eyes were glowing with the excitement of good prospects and the fulfilment of their dreams.

I was also floating gently along that steady stream of people. I nourished the dream of distant Australia in my eyes. A gold mine was reported to have been discovered in that area.

I nourished some other dreams too. A large commercial company with capital assets of about lakhs of rupees was established in that region which eventually monopolised the entire gold industry.

The distant Australia of my dream! The cherished place of my fantasy where wisps of black smoke drifted from the chimneys over the gold mines of Kalgoorlie; the vast sandy plane, thick with shrubs and bushes where the nomadic herdsmen lost their ways in stormy nights!

Walking along the edges of the road was a large procession of people, comprising bare-bodied, starving beggars, old men and women, children, adolescents, young men and women, healthy and diseased, blind and sighted persons.

'May Allah shower his blessing upon you!'

'God bless you, my son!'

God's blessings and Allah's grace have turned out to be the cheapest thing in the world which can be obtained in exchange for a few paise from the marketplace.

A crippled leper stood leaning against the electric pole—the merchant of Allah's blessings! His wallet was overflowing with the stock of Allah's blessings. He wore a fez on his head the colour of which had faded beyond recognition.

His face was creased with numerous lines of ageing and his eyes looked pale and moist. He draped a torn black coat over his body which was rumpled and dirty and perhaps gathered from some dirty slot of a dustbin.

'Allah shall bless you, my child!'

An old woman, spreading a piece of sackcloth on the pavement, had displayed her stock of goods.

'May Allah bless you with long life!'

The old woman rather dealt in more expansive items

such as the blessing for long life. A few customers before me had already purchased that valued item for long life. The corroded tin bowl, placed before her, contained some coins the sum of which would be three annas at most—the price to be paid for a thousand years of life!

Alas, the uncurrent coin treasured in my torn pocket!

Was it possible to buy the blessings of God or the longevity of thousand years in exchange for a nickel?

A cup of tea is preferable to the bargain!

I could certainly pass that uncurrent coin as the current one to the owner of some tea shops in the darkness of the evening.

I stepped into a narrow alleyway.

How beautiful was the bright, glorious shower of sunlight that poured from the eastern sky and the alluring, cloudless, magnanimous autumn sky that resembled the pious look of a self-absorbed, blushing bride, besotted with the passion for her loving husband!

The early sun slanted through the rooftops, casting long shadows across the desolate alleyway, carpeted with red pebbles.

Perth Harbour of Australia! My cherished dream! The ship eventually left Bombay and anchored in Perth Harbour.

It was drifting along the swirling tides of the vast, limitless Indian Ocean. Swarms of seagulls were fluttering along the pounding surfs above the rolling blue waves and the tiny droplets of water, splashed over the ocean floor, were soothing their weary wings. Such was the beauty of Perth Harbour! The mingled smells of sweat and tobacco, the flavours emanating from unfamiliar bodies, and the relishing aroma of Australia overwhelmed my mind with a strange sensation.

It was Amir Khan Alleyway. On a signboard, hanging on the wall was scrawled 'Amir Khan Alleyway' in coal-tar. It seemed to bear the stamp of twentieth-century immortality. In the subcontinent where one can buy thousand years of long life in exchange for a mere two-anna uncurrent coin, a tin board and a lump of coal-tar are enough to ensure ageless immortality for Mr Amir Khan!

'Haven't you ever come across the axiom, Mr Amir Khan, bearded fellow, that one day, everything, including your life and youthfulness, fame and wealth, power and position will be washed away by the pounding waves of time?'

Ha-ha-ha! Perth Harbour and Amir Khan Alleyway. What a coincidence!

Ha-ha-ha!

There were drains on either side of the road. A stream of dirty water was gently flowing along the drains. A dead kitten, scraps of newspaper, straws, and garbage were floating down the skin-deep water of the drain.

A ludicrous mockery of the Indian Ocean!

The foamy lather, issuing from bathrooms and floating along the stream, was creating the illusion of crashing surf, produced by the booming waves on the brimming ocean floor. A swarthy, sickly, ugly-looking, skinny, young lad was rummaging jocundly through that dirty drain water. He was perhaps the child of some poor Dalit, living in the nearby slum areas. Good heavens, what would be more tragic than this hellish torment?

I roared with laughter, derisively, at the sudden discovery.

The lad gave a nervous start and gaped at my face. His pale, fearful eyes glowed with anticipation and excitement.

Even in this twentieth century, a lot of things were yet to be explored by the people. With the growth of industrialisation, some new trades had also been introduced to the commercial sector of India.

The blessing of long life and the endowment of God's grace were a few among them. The Dalit lad's rummaging along the drain was another. Somewhere in the sewage sludge might be hidden a safety pin, a blunt knife, or many such articles and usable. On certain days, when God showered his grace abundantly on the lad, a four-anna or eight-anna coin could be recovered from that dirty drain.

All these were unexplored facts about India.

The uncurrent coin slipped down through my torn pocket and rolled away. I went forward without taking any pause. Let the uncurrent coin be lost in the endless current of the crowd! I found myself caught up in a maelstrom of strange emotions and excitement.

The uncurrent nickel jingled on hitting the ground, producing an unpleasant noise that pierced the weird calmness of the alleyway. Lifting himself instantly from the drain, the lad grabbed the coin like an eagle pouncing upon its prey.

His pair of eyes glowed with the pleasure and satisfaction of success.

He stared at me in shocked amazement. Every corner of his eyes was filled with hatred and distrust in the anticipation that I might snatch that prized piece away from his hand. Suddenly, he put the coin in his mouth and ran off like a terrified victim fleeing from a powerful predator.

At the far end of Amir Khan Alleyway was situated Scavenger Street.

The lad stood on the veranda of a dilapidated hut

on the street. The ground was covered with a thick carpet of white blossom, falling ceaselessly from the Sanjana tree in front of the hut. A feast for the eyes! Standing carelessly on the veranda, he was smoking a bidi with great relish.

On spotting me, the lad disappeared behind the dilapidated mess of the hut. The cherished dream of golden Australia was lost amidst the wilderness of that dilapidated hut on Scavenger Street. Alas, Australia!

It was 2 o'clock in the night. The moon looked lacklustre. But sleep eluded my curious eyes.

Australia . . . the golden Australia . . . the distant Australia, alas!

If I ever write a full chapter on any mortal of this world in my autobiography, he is indisputably Nasir, the cigarette vendor who foolishly sells me cigarettes on credit.

I drew a cigarette from my pocket, lit it up, and began to saunter back towards Amir Khan Alleyway. It was difficult to ignore that remote attraction.

I reached Scavenger Street again. The poor Dalit had peacefully drifted off into sleep in God's dusty lap.

The same Sanjana tree!

The dark shadow of the Sanjana tree crept across the ground in the moonlight slanting through the open spaces between the distant buildings.

The Dalit boy that I met in the afternoon lay sprawled on a piece of sackcloth under the Sanjana tree. A streak of pale moonlight illuminated his dirty body.

It was a beautiful, calm evening. The moon was shining softly, showering its sparks of kindness over the wounded world.

The soothing touch of the evening lulled him into a restful sloth as he ruminated over the fateful events of the passing day.

He would wake up again to the same familiar morning tomorrow and busy himself in his crazed treasure hunt in those dirty drains by Amir Khan Alleyway.

Still, there was no sleep in my weary eyes.

Australia . . . the dream of golden Australia was falling apart like a house of cards before my sleep-deprived eyes.

I stumbled over the bed of sand under the Sanjana tree on which the lad was sleeping peacefully. He held that uncurrent four-anna coin in his delicate hand shining in the night's faint light. A soft laughter line began to swim across his fearful, quivering lips.

I went away.

The moon, behind a patch of clouds, looked pale and lustreless like the uncurrent four-anna coin.

Undefeated

Shyamal finished his bidi when he realised that drawing in more smoke would only deposit black, salivated nicotine.

He went to the window and flicked the stub outside. The warm rays of the setting sun were gradually fading in the fluid darkness of the evening above the distant horizon of the western sky.

But it was very dark and gloomy inside. Shyamal paced up and down inside the dark room. There was no more bidi in his pocket to smoke.

Leela came in carrying a lantern in her hand. She placed the lantern on the table and stood supporting it, like the big-hipped Western actress Marilyn Monroe, looking at the engulfing gloom outside. Lying scattered on the table were some books, notepads, empty tea cups, and the likes that looked messy and chaotic.

Shyamal suddenly peered at Leela and queried, 'Will you say something Leela?' Leela returned her glance from outside and looked earnestly at Shyamal. Perhaps she had got a lot of things to share with Shyamal but could speak nothing on the occasion. Possibly, she was paralysed by her inability to communicate or articulate her feelings.

Leela was scarcely adorned with gold ornaments. She

wore only a pair of glass bangles on her wrists and *Sindhoor* smeared over her receding hairline which were the minimal requisites for a married woman.

Some drops of tears rolled down her cheeks as she looked into Shyamal's eyes.

'You need not cry, Leela. Only those people are supposed to shed tears who accept their defeat without any struggle. How could you accept your defeat so easily against the battle of life?

Leela silently wiped the tear from her eyes.

Life is not as easy as mere jugglery of words. To survive on this earth, one has to pay the price of living at every step. But why did Shyamal ignore this modest demand of life? Was this poverty-stricken, dismal, unceremonious life worth living?

Leela was ruminating over several sad facts that had recently informed her life. But she left without saying anything.

Supporting his head on his palms, Shyamal wearily sank into a nearby chair. Life had become remarkably unendurable these days where no pleasure or sense of taste was left. Is this precarious, chaotic, meaningless existence called life? Why is life muddled with the plight of subsistence?

Shyamal dejectedly surveyed the bookshelf on the wall that treasured with care contributions from many intellectuals and wise men of the world. He had spent twenty-five years of his valuable life, collecting these gemstones of wisdom from different places of this insightful world. Any individual would feel proud of that rare collection. But it had never provided him with any means of subsistence to fill his empty stomach.

On another shelf was stored his stock of manuscripts—the ruinous gemstones of his cultivated knowledge!

Why is life greeted with derision then? Why is it plagued with poverty? What is this despondent misery meant for?

Like a lethal scorpion sting, Shyamal was suddenly reminded of the fact that he and Leela were starving since morning. And it came as a fatal blow to his manliness.

Shyamal angrily stormed out of the house and stepped on the highway of the metropolis. On either side of the highway stood tall buildings and stately pleasure domes. The mysterious highway of the sophisticated society! Pursuing their prized dreams of the golden deer, people meandered along this highway in large numbers at each and every moment of the day. And modern civilisation has termed this onrush of the human tide as progress. Acquisition of more and more gold is their sole motive and objective of life. As if, gold has become the absolute and ultimate destination of their valuable lives. But how despicable this worldly life seems! It's effulgent but lustreless, charming but lifeless, beautiful yet utterly heartless!

Oh, but how beautiful is the starlit sky above the towering roofs and domes of the metropolis! How lovely, graceful, and complete it looks! But has any traveller ever happened to discern that magnificent splendour, paying the price for which the entire gold mines of the world would be emptied?

Leela's stomach rumbled with hunger and felt as if a wild animal with its sharp nails was scraping along the walls of her stomach. A tear traced a path down her flushed cheek. Seth . . . contractors! Gold Prospector Limited! Banks . . . Incorporated Lloyd Bank of England! Wholesale Importers & Exporters! Enjoy your glass: Cool and Refreshing! She looked mournful, with eyes moist with tears. Ah, this bulk of the world's billionaires; the wealthy, affluent societies of the modern world! Why has the world lavishly showered them with loads of good fortunes? And why do thousands of poverty-stricken, pauperised, dreaming people like them wander around the world as penniless beggars on the endless, vicious path of life?

Perhaps, this grating question would be answered by the ultimate gleam of expectation that would kindle the great revolution of posterity. Suddenly a new model Cadillac car slowed down and stood before Shyamal. A bulky, fashionable young man, affecting the latest trends and mannerisms, got down from the driver's seat and shook hands with Shyamal, greeting him good evening.

Shyamal glared at the man in amazement and said, 'Saroj! You're here?'

'I got an excellent, high-paying job in Colombia Gold Prospectors Company, bro! After a quite long time, I'm seeing you again. How far will you go? The office of the *Messenger*, I suppose? Get into my car. I'll drop you there.'

Shyamal and Saroj got into the car and took their seats.

Saroj started up the car's engine and cruised past a turning through the neighbourhood.

'You're a hypocrite, Saroj!'

'Hypocrite?'

'Of course, you are! said Shyamal. 'In the final battle between talent and wealth, ultimately you succumbed to the temptation of wealth betraying your innate talent. You might have gained some personal benefit from it, but you have undermined the spirit of talent in general by bowing your head before the insolent pressure of wealth.'

Saroj could not readily give an appropriate explanation for this scurrilous accusation as he steered his car through a busy area of the city. Taking a turn down the main street, he said,

'Talent has lost the battle against wealth since long, Shyamal and this defeat is not personal that has influenced my life. It has occurred worldwide. Talent has become a slave to wealth and property! That apart, a person should not boast about his talent when he already sets out for an ideal renunciation.'

Leela's tearful face suddenly flashed through Shyamal's sensitive mind. He was again reminded of the fact that they had not taken any food since last night. His disgraced, humiliated, hunger-stricken manliness could not raise any protest against these hard facts of life. Leaning out of the car window, he was only noiselessly peering at the busy public moving along the crowded street.

This part of the city was particularly known for the residences of many affluent people of the metropolis. The towering height of these tall buildings on either side of the road was rivalling the soaring sky, as if.

The troops of talent are held captive behind the walls of these secure citadels, erected by the mighty enemy force. The enemy possesses huge armies of trained soldiers, equipped with an infinite number of deadly armaments. And what these troops of talent are left with? Alas, this ignoble, dismal, insignificant, feeble, penniless, and bereft talent persists in struggling against an invincible opponent!

Saroj pulled one cigarette from his costly cigarette case and stuck it between his lips. Then he passed a cigarette to Shyamal. A cold inertness had crept over Shyamal's body and mind for want of smoke since last evening. Shyamal quickly lit a cigarette and took a puff.

The office of the *Messenger* stood by the main road.

Saroj's car halted. Giving a mild thank, Shyamal got down from the car.

*

The editor of the *Messenger* named Mr Mrinmay was an illustrious, successful, and affluent man who happened to be a friend of Shyamal. Hence, he did not face much difficulty in meeting him. But many wretched, frustrated talents, at that time, had deliberately crowded outside the waiting room for an appointment with Mr Mrinmay.

Seeing them, a despairing sigh shuddered through Shyamal's body. These unfortunate fellows represented the sovereign power of talent and had possessed the utmost courage to manifest their latent potential. Yet, after being defeated, they now arrived at the camp of wealth to sign the treaty of peace.

How absurd is this precarious battle between talent and wealth? Let the greatest battle of the millennium be ended here in this blessed place. Talent has undeniably lost its austere grandeur today. It has now reached the threshold of wealth, screaming and begging for mercy.

Shyamal hurried into Mrinmay's office room. Mrinmay, at that moment, was glancing through the headlines of the *Messenger*, freshly published that evening.

'Please, be seated!' said Mrinmay.

Then he paused to open his cigarette case and offered it to Shyamal.

Shyamal lit up a cigarette and said, 'I have finally turned up, Mrinmay.'

'That's good,' said Mrinmay.

'I have no hesitation to perform whatever assignment you give to me,' said Shyamal.

Mrinmay bumped into the swivel chair and stretched his feet up on the table, 'Good, very good!'

'I'm not joking, Mrinmay.'

'Look Shyamal,' said Mrinmay. 'You possessed an extraordinary talent in writing profiles of eminent and distinguished persons. I want you to prepare a profile of the business tycoon and billionaire Mr K. to be published in the morning edition of the *Messenger*. This done, he would be pleased to buy a share of about lakhs of rupees from one of my companies.'

'I have no objection, Mrinmay,' said Shyamal. 'I'll send it to you in two or three days. I'm grateful to you for this act of kindness.'

'Oh! What are you saying, Shyamal?' Mrinmay said in a patronising voice, grinning cheerfully. 'I don't like these useless formalities, you know.'

And then, Mrinmay passed him a cheque and said, 'This is your remuneration in advance, brother, on behalf of the *Messenger*. I want you to write one profile every week to fill the column of my newspaper.'

Shyamal quickly skimmed through the cheque which was for a sum of one thousand rupees. The sturdy iron shackles of bondage quickly fell over the wrist and feet of the proud talent, oppressively weighing him down to a hellish torment!

Shyamal bade his farewell and stepped out of the office room.

*

Three days passed.

A parcel, sent from Shyamal, reached Mrinmay's office. Perhaps it contained the profile as requested by Mrinmay. He elatedly opened the parcel. But to his utter surprise, he found some blank sheets of paper inside it on which were scribbled some triangles, rectangles, light marks of crosses, and a series of straight and curved lines. The cheque for one thousand rupees and a letter written by Shyamal were cautiously enclosed with the sheets of paper:

Dear Mrinmay, I owe you an apology. For the last three days, I tried my best to prepare the write-up as desired by you, but I could not.

In my opinion, the greatest battle of the millennium is not the one that is waged between two national powers or doctrines, but between wealth and talent. Talent always seeks to prevail over wealth and prestige and to utilise them as a means to its cherished goal. Similarly, wealth seeks to seize hold of talent and use it as a means to its prized end. This battle between wealth and talent has proliferated throughout the entire world. The troops of talent have escaped from the battlefield and the brave generals have retired to their respective safer havens. Many a rival of wealth has also been sold into slavery under the influence of wealth. But I must continue to fight the battle till the last breath of my life. I'm undefeated.

Mrinmay crumpled up the letter, threw it to the wastebasket, and pressed the calling button intolerantly, overwrought with undue excitement.

First Rain of the Monsoon

It was an evening in the month of Ashadha. Heavy rain squalls began to fill the evening of the early monsoon.

A stream of muddy water was meandering along the desolate street.

My boots were sodden and heavy, with water burbling around them. And the raincoat was tattered and damn old.

The shirt under my raincoat was drenched by rain showers.

This part of the town looked deserted and comparatively less crowded. On both sides of the road stood tall, sky-kissing buildings of the affluent and aristocratic people. Streaming through the windows of the upper floor, the dim light of the electric lamps was glistening along the dusty path.

The first rain of the monsoon was pouring down heavily against the hard surface. It was restless, discontented, and interminable.

I could not see the face of the girl in the darkness. But, of course, the face of the young, man standing beside her, was partially visible in the light, streaming from the nearby house. Perhaps they wanted to spend all their time together, either talking or making love—the secret romance of showering early monsoon.

The young man curled his arms softly around the girl's slender waist.

The evening was getting denser and more sombre over time. It was still raining heavily. And carried along the unruly wind, droplets of rain shower lashed against the girl's elegant forehead. What was her name? Urvashi? Menaka? Rambha? The man occasionally was kissing on her wet head, and sucking the cold rainwater cascading from her forehead with great relish. Everything looked elegant and beautiful.

'Swine,' I blurted out.

Having been drenched completely in rain showers, they were rushing madly towards me in the dark and accidentally knocked into my side.

They were husband and wife and worked as coolies to earn their livelihood. Perhaps they were returning home after their day's hard work. They did not apologise to me. Neither did they pay any heed to my sudden scream. Rushing madly about, they finally merged in the immersing darkness of the evening.

I too could not apologise to them but my conscience did.

A morbid, insatiable curiosity prompted me to overhear their conversation. I went under the window of the two-storied building to listen in on their private gossip, hiding under the cover of the engulfing darkness.

'Anybody there?'

Then I heard what sounded like an aged man coughing and hacking in the distance. I found an old man reclining on the wall. I couldn't see his face in the dark. One of his daughters was sitting near him, burying her face between her knees. Both of them had taken shelter beside the wall to prevent themselves from the heavy rain shower.

The soft conversation of the couple was sounded from upstairs.

'Beautiful!'

'What beautiful?'

'You and the rain squalls.'

Then followed the familiar sound of repeated kissing which only persisted in my inference, not in my experience.

How many times had I asked you to return home early as the rain clouds began to gather in the darkening sky,' the uncouth girl screamed at the old man. 'But you remained unmoved. Now you must pay for your carelessness and spend the whole night under some stranger's thatch eaves.'

'But who could have a handle on the rain squalls, daughter?' the old man responded with a series of broken coughs. 'It was rushing like anything and covered the entire place in no time. Please give me a cheroot if you have got one.'

'Cheroot or fire,' the girl yelled out at him.

'Don't be angry my daughter. It doesn't make sense to get angry when one cannot even manage to eat twice a day,' said the old man as a racking cough convulsed his whole body.

Oh, how ignoble was their poverty! I left the place instantly with seething resentment. I was not able to hear the rain-spattered, amorous strain of the early monsoon any more amidst their noisy quarrel.

As I walked some distance, I suddenly felt like going back to the homeless destitute and offering my delayed apology to them.

But I had moved a long distance ahead.

It was somebody's drawing room. An attractive, well-furnished, brightly lighted room, filled with the flavours of cigarette smoke. The teacups on the table were glittering in the light of the electric lamps. Some garrulous people were sitting around the table. Their bald heads glinted in the lights streaming through the windows.

A rickshaw passed through the desolate street in the rain. The rickshaw puller's head and waist created a perfect right angle. The lines in his face had contracted and his teeth were madly chattering against one another from cold. The rickshaw was moving steadily without pause.

'India became independent, and I am pretty sure something is going to happen this time on this side or that.'

'Long live independent India!'

The opening of soda bottles sounded from the drawing room on the edge of the road. And clinks of glasses echoed awkwardly throughout the room.

'Long live independent India!'

The rickshaw disappeared near a turning in the distance. I was suddenly overcome by an uncontrollable desire to apologise to the rickshaw puller. But he had already vanished from sight.

The rain had not abated yet but it was gradually reducing to a fine drizzle.

The tuneful melody of a lyre playing with a soft female voice resonated from the nearby two-storied building.

Which raga was she singing the song in? Was it Purabi? Darbari Kanada? Bagesri? Malhar?

It seemed unfamiliar to my knowledge.

But it was really beautiful. Everything around me looked graceful, pleasant, and fascinating. The only thing which looked ugly and unpleasant was poverty. Hideous, menacing poverty! The house nearby was owned by one of my friends. I went inside.

Amidst the usual hubbub of the household, my friend had just returned from an outing. He was thoroughly drenched in rainwater. The whole household had become agitated over this trifling issue. Sister Surama had yet to get the napkin which was lost somewhere in the house. And what heinous charges the servant was reprimanded with over the issue of the lost napkin! Lalita, my friend's wife was also so busy with her unremitting daily chores. The cook had not prepared the tea yet. My friend's mother was also not less busy with her daily work.

She complained to me about my friend's obstinate behaviour, 'Do you see, my son, how stubborn has he grown these days! Won't he fall ill by soaking in rain showers? Has the tea prepared yet?'

'Just serving, Mother,' responded the cook from inside.

'He is a beast, not a man,' said Lalita as the cook appeared with two cups of hot tea.

The beast-man cook carried the ingredients of tea on a tray and placed it on a fanciful tea table before Lalita.

Lalita prepared the tea. Binod's mother lifted herself from the chair. And sister Surama again busied herself examining the things that were saturated by the rain showers.

Binod took a noisy slurp of his tea and exclaimed, 'What a wonderful tea, Lalita! You deserve a reward for this.'

But who had actually prepared the tea—the beast-man cook or the earth-bound fairy Lalita? Binod was doing injustice. Let him do it!

'Tell then, what you can do for me,' asked Lalita shyly, blushing a little, and glancing downward. A faint smile swam across her thin, quivering lips.

'Listen,' said Binod.

Lalita lifted herself and sportively came closer to Binod, and stood near him.

'Bow your head,' said Binod.

Bowing her conch-white neck, Lalita stood noiselessly near Binod. Binod groped in his pocket and instantly tucked a bud of *kadamba* flower in her locks of hair.

Lalita went inside with a winning smile, waving her thick, long braid in the air. The pleasing fragrance of the *kadamba* flower began to permeate the humid air of the house.

I was about to finish my tea when my friend said, 'Gosh, your clothes were thoroughly sodden!'

I roared with laughter.

Sodden clothes, sodden soil, and a passionless, frigid Earth! Like the late-night lovemaking of an old lady. I went away.

It was a modest hut on Coolie Street. My rented house was situated at a small distance from here. The door was half-opened. Somebody lay sprawled on the bare floor covering his entire body in a tattered quilt. A lamp-wick was flickering in the dark room casting warm yellow light all around. All traces of life had vanished from the lonely hut. I left the place.

It again started pouring with freezing rain. Let it pour continually and without interruption! Let the entire sky be emptied of any sign of rain clouds!

*

The entire room including my bed was drenched as heavy showers of rain had flurried through the open window.

The saturated, shrunken, cold, and frigid Earth of the first monsoon! And the wet, cold, and forsaken bed!

Sleep eluded my eyes.

I was walking back and forth desultorily around the room. It was precisely fourteen steps as I measured my strides from this side to that.

How admirable were Binod's mother, wife, and sister, and yet how selfish were they? They were affectionate but intolerant. Generous but mean. In contrast to them, the beast-man cook seemed quite healthy, sturdy, and reliable. The scene of the gaunt, old man, sheltering by the drain alongside the road with her quarrelsome daughter, and the obsessed beloved, in the crepuscular light of the evening, whose forelock was continually adorned by millions of cascading gems by the showering raindrops, suddenly flashed through my mind in the enveloping darkness. The swarm of baldheads enjoying themselves over a cup of tea in the drawing room, and the happy couple in the dark whom I reprimanded by calling 'swine' began to trip down my memory lane.

And again, the memory of that poor rickshaw puller whose head and waist had created a perfect right angle, and the rain-drenched *kadamba* flower, adorning the locks of Lalita's beautiful hair remained etched in my curious mind.

It was again fourteen steps from this side to that, but I stopped at the twelfth step to lit up a cigarette.

To my surprise, the cigarette was sodden and the glued heads of the matchsticks were washed away by the rain showers.

The ground outside was soggy by the first rains of the monsoon. It was beautiful yet unpleasant, graceful yet cruel, fascinating yet shrunken... a frigid, wet evening like the warm embrace of a languishing elderly lady!

The Editor

It was the office of the *Swadesh*—a local newspaper. The chamber of the editor was situated at a secluded place on the second floor of the building. The floor was spread with expensive carpets. In the middle of the chamber stood one large secretariat table. Some extravagant cushioned chairs were neatly furnished around the table. The editor was seated on a moving chair. Innumerable books were crammed inside the glass almirahs by the sides of the walls surrounding the chamber. The growing clamour of the ground floor did not reach the lonesome chamber of the editor. It was locked from the inside.

The bright sun of the day was gradually sinking into the ocean of blood in the western sky. The light of the day was slaying the darkness of the evening. Nay—the darkness of the evening was slaying the light of the day. Perhaps, each was engaged in murdering the other in cold blood. A bloody battle between the light and the darkness ensued in the serene sky of the evening. Yet, how tranquil was the placid world below? How peaceful it seemed! No, no—how fierce was the world below, filled with gruesome skirmishes, awful noise, and macabre unrest! But, if the world was devoid of these skirmishes, noise, and unrest, wouldn't he be employed in some modest business such as grass cutting instead of preparing news reports? Oh, how could he forget that his job was to supply the so-called elites of the society with the news of all battles, agitations, and unrests of the world and to plunder all beauty, peacefulness, and serenity of human life! Wasn't it his mission to enamel falsehood with the gloss of truth and to exaggerate it beyond the limit?

The telephone rang out.

It rang several times and then stopped ringing.

It rang many times today like this and finally stopped ringing. The editor did not choose to pick up the phone.

Today, in the morning edition of the *Swadesh* was published in big bold letters, "Mr Shree's Extramarital Relation: Secret Meeting with a Lady." Mr Shree was a political leader and a rival of the patronising leader of the *Swadesh*. Hence, the report was published to tarnish Shree's reputation in society and to force him into a self-imposed exile from the field of political rivalry.

Perhaps it was Shree who had been making repeated phone calls to the office of the *Swadesh* to protest this malicious falsehood.

The music of a violin being played by a famous ustad was sounded from a radio in a nearby house. The unceremonious setting of the sun in the distant western sky bore a strong connection with this warm violin music. It was poignant, and touching, but beautiful. As if, the volatile, azure streams of life were immolating themselves in the whirlpool of the sea of futility! That self-immolation looked very pathetic, yet inspired both pity and amusement.

The electric lamps inside the office rooms were lighted. The editor opened the sealed envelope placed on the table for a long time and quickly skimmed through the letter. It was a secret letter sent by the patronising political leader. Another report about

Shree was required to be published with the title, 'Mr Shree's Soliciting Funds from the Capitalists of the Foreign Countries.' The report had to be published without fail in the morning edition tomorrow as the election dates were drawing near.

The telephone rang out again and again and then stopped ringing.

The editor left his chair and began to pace up and down inside the chamber. The bloody civil war between the light and the darkness was over on the distant horizon. A twinkling bright star of the evening appeared above the foliage of the pine tree to sign the treaty of peace.

The telephone rang again. The editor now picked up the receiver and listened in. It was the patronising political leader himself.

'I had rung you up around twenty times today,' the leader complained.

'I didn't pick up the phone expecting them to be Mr Shree's calls,' replied the editor.

'Look, Mr Shree has to be systematically slaughtered as a rule,' said the political leader. 'Yeah, herein lies the merit of adult education! You do not require a gun or a knife any longer to kill your rival. That method of killing has become obsolete. Many wicked Caesar can be killed at mere pen point in the blink of an eye. The new and most powerful weapon of modern civilisation!'

'Sir,' responded the editor.

'You must have received my letter,' enquired the political leader. 'Please ensure that the report is published in the morning edition. Again, it's desirable to publish an editorial remark on the matter so that there would be no other option left for Mr Shree except suicide or self-imposed exile.'

'But if he lodges a defamation case against us?' the editor queried.

'Huh,' snorted the political leader and said, 'You have got unprecedented wealth and money with the Swadesh Company Pvt. Ltd.'

The editor put the receiver down and returned to his seat in a dejected mood. Shree's old, innocent, becalmed face began to float before his mind's eye. The editor had nothing to worry about if Shree had called him several times to lodge his protest about the falsehood. But this silent protest seemed louder and sharper than ever. Yet, it was not truth but mere silence which came into protesting this grave injustice.

The hawkers on the street would have shouted, bursting out their chests, advertising the title of the report, concerning Shree's extramarital affair. And perhaps, Shree would have bought a newspaper for himself perusing which his innermost soul would have screamed out in an inexpressible, excruciating torment like a wounded bird . . . Oh, God!

The third crescent of the new moon rose above the pine tree at a distance. The editor gazed at that silver crescent moon for a moment. Floating above the hushed, noiseless pine tree, it looked like Shashilekha, adorning the matted-hair curls of Lord Nataraja, exactly after his strenuous tandava. How elegantly it manifested its spectral beauty in this imperfect world! What sublime expression of truth! Yet, guided by that standard of beauty and truth, nobody on this sinful earth would have observed the scenic beauty of that crescent moon above the pine tree today. And if observed, they might not be able to measure the depth of this fascinating beauty. Else, there would be no necessity for the *Swadesh* in contemporary society.

The editor groped for a pen in his pocket and started writing a brief note—the last note of his life:

The third crescent of the new moon is sinking below the ocean of the twilit sky. Serenity comes unsolicited like an uninvited guest and knocks at the threshold of people's closed houses. But the guardians of the houses are just transfixed by the warmth of uninterrupted prosperity. Serenity proudly departs in the darkness of the night with a wounded conscience. And mighty wails of nightmares billow out from the innumerable feathery beds of prosperity. Prosperity has become the most tempting thing in the world, not serenity. But prosperity sans serenity is like the luxurious feast of sumptuous foods by a patient with chronic dyspepsia.

Everybody in the present world pine for absolute power. In the guise of professing patriotism, nobody in the present society holds themselves back from consolidating power to commit the most loathsome crime in the world. Yet the aim of all such struggles is peace, the object of all such sins is virtue.

This, perhaps, is the only message issued by the descending crescent to the depraved world stricken with infinite self-deception.

The editor finished his writing and rose from the chair. Before leaving his office, he tore off the freshly written report on Mr Shree and threw it to the bin, containing bits of waste paper. Then he prepared himself to go home. Most days, he used to forget to take his staff with him while leaving his chamber for home in the evening. But today, after such a long time, he did not forget to take his staff with him. Who knows, he might not require coming back to the office any longer from tomorrow.

*

It was the evening of the next day.

A grand public meeting was convened in the assembly hall of the town. Mr Shree sat dejectedly at one corner of the podium. The meeting continued uninterrupted. The assembly hall was crammed with people who came from far and near to listen to their favourite political leaders. The leader finally ended his speech amidst a hearty round of loud applause. And then, at the request of the president, Mr Shree rose from his seat to deliver a speech. Another huge applause began to ripple around the podium when one hawker of the *Swadesh* from behind cried out at the audience about Shree's extramarital affair, published in the morning edition of the *Swadesh* yesterday. Without delay, the crowd began to pelt Mr Shree with loads of rotten eggs and coal tar. Mr Shree somehow managed to sneak back behind the podium to save his life.

The editor noticed everything, sitting amongst the audience. The enraged avatar of people grieved him a great deal as though thousands of needles were pricking all over his bare body. The civilised, scientific man of the 20th century has deliberately replaced the five-headed Lord Brahma with a headless human god. And this human god possesses no head or brain and hence persists without judgment and conscience. Following this principle, their notion of mathematics is completely new and different from that of ours. As per our mathematical principles, the sum of one and one is equal to two. But according to theirs, the result of the addition of one man to another is a negative man. And when they are added in groups, they emerge as individuals without conscience or human qualities. Headless shoulders! Like God who complies with the wishes of his sincere devotees, so also, these human gods remain in complicity with their sincere devotees. But, when these human gods perform the vigorous dance of tandava, humanity is banished from this beautiful world. The words that come out from their blessed mouths assume the status of God's dictate. Those who do not comply with that dictate are charged with serious crimes like treason and miserably fail to secure their place in society.

Perhaps this explains the reason why Shree was pelted with loads of rotten eggs and coal tar—a cruel curse issued by the human gods.

There is no dearth of people like political leaders, servile bards, news reporters and editors in the world who remain forever loyal and devoted to these sovereign human gods with great sycophantic subservience.

*

A few days after . . .

The night rolled on. The cursed, banished Mr Shree was seated on a bench at a desolate spot on the riverbank.

Having wandered around the lonely places near the riverbank, the former, unemployed editor of the *Swadesh*, finally appear at that place and took his seat beside Mr Shree.

A lack-lustre, freakish moon of the dark fortnight was shining faintly behind the capricious clouds.

'Who are you,' asked Mr Shree.

'I am the editor,' replied the editor of the *Swadesh*.

'What are you doing here at this advanced hour of the night?' enquired Mr Shree.

'I am chewing nuts,' said the editor. 'And you?'

'I am taking fresh air,' said Mr Shree.

'Both are good for health,' The editor remarked.

After some awkward moments of silence, Mr Shree blurted out, 'I think the human-gods are needed to be worshipped with elaborate rites and rituals.'

'I too am fed up with chewing nuts for quite a long period,' replied the editor. 'I would be happy to sit with you on the worshipping dais to chant hymns of praise to the human gods. I have learnt them all by heart.'

'Then the human gods will be greatly pleased with our effort,' said Mr Shree rather enthusiastically. 'For this reason, I want to publish a daily newspaper. Will you be the editor of that local newspaper?'

'Wonderful!' exclaimed the editor. 'I am ever prepared for that.'

'Do you know what I would like to publish in the very first issue of that newspaper?' enquired Mr Shree.

'Netaji's female feticide,' the editor replied with a glowing face.

Mr Shree grabbed the editor at once and clasped him tightly to his bosom, overcome by a novel sensation. 'And then, he would be left with no option except wandering around futilely and cracking nuts with his teeth.'

Mr Shree burst into loud peals of laughter invaded by a plethora of emotions and excitements.

The ugly, deformed moon of the dark fortnight was secretly hiding behind an array of shredded clouds. As if the darkening firmament was busy chucking its preposterous debris into the lofty wastebasket made from the broken, shredded clouds.

The human god's world of beauty and truth also seemed as absurd, ugly and lifeless as the preposterous debris of this indifferent sky.

Mr Shree once again burst into loud peals of laughter . . . a relentless mockery of the notions of truth and beauty by an eminent human god.

Ward No. 17

It was difficult to tell the exact time of the day.

It had been pouring with rain continually since yesterday night. Nilakantha Pattnaik woke up early in the morning and started reciting his devotional song namely, 'Raghupati Raghaba Raja Ram' by himself.

The other three were still fast asleep, lying lazily on their dirty bed, covering their bodies from head to toe with a shabby blanket. The iron gate of Ward No. 17 was open for a long time. The warder of the prison was dozing off, reclining wearily on the inner wall of the ward, to prevent himself from the flurrying rain shower since early morning. The vicinity of the prison began to be resonated with the noise of the third-class prisoners performing their daily penal labour. Curling columns of smoke emitted from the gaping rooftop, slabbed with burnt clay tiles.

Balaram was a C-class hardened criminal. He would reach here after some time, carrying hot tea in a large kettle. The sleep-stricken body instantly became animated with the prospect of the smoky tea. Some disconnected thoughts of the last night began to stir up in the troubled mind: With what criminal charges have they arrested me and confined me like a bullock in this pinfold prison cell? What crime have

I committed against this human society and civilisation? Unfortunately, I have not been informed of that fact yet.

But what punishment is prescribed for this heinous crime? A greyish-brown jeep halted in front of my house. A police inspector sprang out of the jeep and said, 'You're under arrest. You have to come with me just now.' I followed his order and took my seat inside the jeep. The jeep stopped before a prison house. Then the iron gates of the prison began to close, one after one, behind my back. How inhuman, hideous, and vulgar is this human civilisation! Perhaps this sanctioned vulgarity prevalent in our human society is called civilisation.

Sudam was a B-class criminal hailed from the princely state of Athagarh. Squatting down on the moistened floor, he was busy sweeping the room clean with a broom. He was clad in a white shirt and a half pant with thick tracks as prescribed for the B-class criminal in an Indian prison. He had stuck one-fourth of a bidi behind his ear. He was a burglar who broke into people's houses for theft. But, if theft is a crime, then who is the criminal—the man who steals or the man who hoards wealth?

Nilakantha Pattnaik finished his recitation of devotional songs. His face looked bright and cheerful. He was a sixty-year-old man. But there was not even a faint trace of lethargy or weariness visible in his face or mind. The rain finally began to ease off. Slowly, the eastern sky was being cleared of its blemishes as clouds began to disperse from it.

A dove couple, in some invisible, dark corner of their nest, started humming a cheerful note that filled the cloudy morning with a pleasing sensation. How strange are they and their soulful melody! I have heard their love songs, resonating on the top of the temples, on the dome of the mosques, on the church tower, in the police court and in and outside the house. And today, I heard that song from the confined corner of this prison cell. As if this sweet, passionate melody and its rich profusion are the ultimate truth of human life which is beyond society and civilisation, vice and virtue, piety and impiety.

Balaram hurried in, carrying a large kettle, brimming with hot tea. Wearing his sodden clothes, Balaram has gone out in search of a pinch of tobacco on this cloudy morning. Sitting down in that small room, now he may be engaged in a conversation with driver Ram about the pain and pleasure of a modest living with the intent of getting some tobacco from him. How smart, sly and manipulative this driver Ram is! God knows, how he manages to bring tobacco inside the prison. Perhaps it is the eighth wonder of the world. Balaram left after pouring hot tea into a brass bowl. I lit up a cigarette and lifted the brass bowl to my lips.

It is strange to note how society and civilisation have changed. Even the last penny of the treasury is believed to be spent on the restoration of truth and justice in this society. The self-restraint, exhibited in the characters of the civilised socialites in agitating the entire world, is termed as patriotism, valour and glory by this human society. And this Ward No. 17 is a silent witness to all such corrupt practices and irregularities and how the wealth of the nation is being continually looted in the name of restoring peace and discipline by trampling one's liberty for another's benefit, suppressing the genuine truth and justice of the human world.

No sooner does a child become familiar with the alphabet, he is taught always to speak the truth and never to tell a lie.

Yet, that child, when in its mature age, learns to speak the truth, the iron gate of Ward No. 17 begins to close behind his back.

'Sacrifice your life for the sake of truth and justice.' —

who on earth is not familiar with this common precept? But when the real struggle begins to uphold that truth and justice, one has to face the onslaught of police and judges at every step. And they meticulously accomplish their aims in the name of establishing truth and justice in society. Ward No. 17 was a silent and dumb witness to all such depraved activities.

'Let's puff on a cigarette.'

'Cigarette! No, Babu . . . we are even not allowed to talk to the prisoners,' said the warder, rubbing the sleep from her slightly swollen eyes.

It stopped raining. I again offered him a cigarette, 'You can take one now, please. Nobody is around.'

The warder put the cigarette to his lips and lit it up. Then wreathed in blue cigarette smoke, he transferred himself into a fairly gregarious chap.

'You know, Babu,' the warder began. 'I was recruited to this job during the Salt March. These ministers of today have suffered a great deal of torment at that cursed time. One day, the evening bell rang, announcing the prisoners to return to their respective wards. Earlier, one senior minister along with about thirty members of his party had been crammed into these two tiny wards. They kept on insisting, 'We shall no longer be detained inside the wards even from the evening time.' The prison officials tried their best to pacify the throng but to no avail. And then, the whistle sounded. A troop of around sixty warders armed with rifles and lathis rushed to the spot. Seeing the armed warders, they instantly crossed their arms before their chests and lay down flat, covering their faces against the ground. Streams of blood began to fill the dusty ground as a result of random bayonet stabbings and lathi charges. Some of them lost consciousness and others persisted. We carried them back inside the wards by our shoulders and locked the wards.

Then we returned to our reserve, holding our fixed bayonets and lathis, splattered with viscous blood. I could not sleep the whole night that day. I wondered as to why they suffered such hellish torment. What crime were they accused of? Is fighting for freedom a sin?'

'But fighting for freedom, at that time, as the aristocratic people of that society believed, was a detestable, heinous crime,' the warder added.

'And today?' I queried.

The head constable of the prison was about to arrive. The warder quickly slipped into his raincoat and went away.

The evening sky looked clear and spotless. A strange liveliness had animated the wind. A few prisoners including myself pleaded before the constable not to lock us inside the ward before 9 in the night. We did not like to stay in confinement like herd-bound cattle as quickly as from the early evening. Seeing our insistence, the constable immediately called upon the head constable and complained about our non-compliance. The head constable advised and threatened the prisoners not to go against the rule, 'The outcome of your repeated insistence may not be good, I warn.' Perhaps we were destined to be flogged until our backs were bloody like the one that happened 18 years back. But I persisted in not to have been locked inside the ward before 9. The head constable finally called on the jailer and reported him about the matter. Jailer Sahib reached the place soon. An unnatural crudeness and perplexity had informed his demeanour: How come a mere prisoner displayed such boldness of temper?

The jailer issued an ultimatum, demanding me to comply with the order, 'Bear in mind that your decision can lead you to some serious consequence.'

The irresistible calmness and effervescence of the

evening had disappeared amidst this crude and offensive warning. We returned to our ward with silent steps. What would have happened if we persisted with our decision? Maybe again that whistle would have sounded. The warders would have rushed to that place from the reserve and then returned with their blood-splattered lathis. And if one among them had happened to be a bit emotional, sleep would have eluded his eyes for the whole night.

But why do these injustices still haunt us today? All such prisoners of the pre-independent era have now become powerful leaders of the state upon whom depend the entire fate of the nation. Hadn't they suffered in their pulses the agonising pain of that brutish confinement of being banished from the effervescent autumn evening? Then how could they allow such injustices to happen?

Did they have any vested interest in the freedom struggle?

Perhaps the head constable was coming towards us. Somebody knocked at the locked door wall of Ward No. 17 as a warning signal. Watchman Rama, wrapping a cloth around his head, hurried out from the warmth of the jail building. It again started to drizzle. This watchman Rama was a B-class criminal. He hailed from a Dalit Street of a tiny hamlet named Patrapur in Koraput District, surrounded by rolling hills on each side.

It was an advanced hour of the day. Perhaps the dove couple had returned to their loft for the afternoon rest and milled about the ward, softly cooing to each other. A flock of swallows suddenly scurried inside Ward No. 17, chasing after one another, and then merged away amidst the steady drizzle of rain.

Prisoner Dharmu appeared before me for a smoke.

I gave him a cigarette. He extended his sincere gratitude to me and said, 'Do not leave your bed, Babu. The lunch bell will ring just now.' Then sitting on the edge of the bed, he started to press my legs to ward off the laziness of my fatigued body. Ah, how relaxing it felt! How relishing! This Dharmu Naik was an untouchable and a resident of the hilly areas of Anugul. He was being punished for the crime of flogging his wife to death. How easily could he crush a human life to death like insects to wicked boys, and now, how affectionate had he grown, showering his sincere love for a stranger!

I gazed at his strong-built, muscular chest.

Both an animal and a human being had nested there.

Meanwhile, the animal had been banished from the ward. It was the human which persisted. And perhaps this explains why his heart was flooded with such affection, sympathy and best wishes for the common humanity.

Strange was that prison cell. I dragged myself out of bed.

The Dying Dinosaur

Perhaps, the train was moving along the Rupa Bridge.

Maharaja Ray Brajeshwar Ray opened the glazed shutter window of the train and peeped outside. An ashen shower of sunlight began to pour from the eastern sky by degrees. The beautiful morning was approaching like a lady with tears rolling down her white cheeks.

The Maharaja woke up to a pounding headache and a splitting hangover due to the overconsumption of whisky last night.

Yep . . . it was Rupa Bridge. The meandering water of the river Rupa under the bridge slept gloriously on the sandy banks like a woman after the exhausting intercourse of a late night. Was it Madhavi, Mohini, Srimati, or Anuradha?

Brajeshwar lighted his extinguished pipe and began to brood over the changes wrought by time in this long gap of ten years. To his great relief, he found that nothing had changed. Rupa River and the familiar landscape on its bank looked the same as it looked ten years back and wasn't the Raj Kanchangarh station ahead? Nothing was altered indeed.

Ten years was not a long time. Brajeshwar took off his woollen nightgown and threw it on the berth.

The homecoming to Kanchangarh today on this wintry morning after the lapse of ten long years instantly made his mind fresh and lively. The train slowed down after entering the Kanchangarh station yard. Some people on the platform were giving tribute to the Maharaja, laurelled admiring words in unison. Brajeshwar lent his ears to the noise . . . 'Long live Maharaja Ray Brajeshwar Ray!' Brajeshwar's cruel rigid face wrinkled with faint laughter lines.

The train stopped moving. Brajeshwar was listlessly looking at the platform through the window. He was returning to Kanchangarh today after ten long years of exile. Hence, the platform was crammed with people who came to welcome him home. Meanwhile, Kanchangarh was no more regarded as a princely state and the kingship was abolished. The iron body of Brajeshwar was spattered with the rust of senile decay. Brajeshwar flung open the door of his compartment. And then, three of his stewards entered with utmost caution and alacrity. One of them began to drape him in clothes and the other held a water pot and a napkin to wash his face. Another steward approached carrying morning tea on a tray. Throngs of people were bestowing words of praise for the Maharaja, celebrating his return with great pomp and show outside the compartment. The departure of the train from the station was delayed by three minutes. Yet, Brajeshwar had not come out from his coupe. His luggage was being unloaded from another compartment which comprised piles of guns, innumerable boxes and trunks, a few cameras and other items. Brajeshwar alighted from the coupe and walked down the platform with slow steps. The stillness of the morning sky was instantly shattered with tributes and accolades from the people in praise of their Maharaja. Brajeshwar's sober face was not visible any more, now shrouded with the garlands of marigold flowers saturated by the heavy dew of the early morning.

Brajeshwar released a puff of smoke from his pipe and enquired from a man standing near him, 'Hello, Mr Mahapatra! How do you do? Are they all residents of Kanchangarh?'

'Hearing the news that their Lord is coming, they have planted vaulted arches on both sides of the road leading to the station and decorated it with overflowing pitchers, awaiting eagerly your homecoming since dawn,' said Mr Mahapatra. Nilambar Mahapatra.

The memories of that cursed night ten years back suddenly flashed before his eyes. It was a dark ominous night in September 1942. Political agent Mr Michael Sahib muttered drowsily, intoxicated by an overdose of whisky, 'By the order of the sovereign British Government you have to leave Kanchangarh instantly in exile for five years.' Holding their handmade guns and dynamites, a mob of angry protestors outside Kanchangarh Palace was ready to resort to violence and bloodshed against the despotic tyrannical Brajeshwar. It was this Mahapatra, who with his clever stratagem was finally successful in escorting him secretly to Raj Kanchangarh station. Mr Mahapatra used to be inevitably a part of all cruel and fiendish caprices of Brajeshwar in the past. For this reason, he was sentenced to three long years of imprisonment on charges of many atrocious activities.

Mr Mahapatra screamed out loud at the crowd, asking them to disperse and to make room for the Maharaja to proceed.

A red Rolls-Royce motor car parked before the station gate with much difficulty slowly cutting through the huge committed crowds. Brajeshwar took his seat in the car. Mr Mahapatra hurried to the driver's seat and started the engine.

Although there had been a lot of changes visible on Brajeshwar's face, his autocratic slender body, his unruly messy hair that fell over his bleak forehead and the inebriated look in his glittering eyes like the edges of a sharp blade seemed unaltered through the passage of time.

'Drive the car fast Mr Mahapatra. I have to reach Kanchangarh in one hour and 15 minutes,' said Brajeshwar. Kanchangarh was situated 70 miles away from the station, but the car was cruising at a speed of ten miles per hour.

'Sure, sir! But the way people have crowded here, it's almost impossible,' Mr Mahapatra replied as he strived to drive the car a little faster.

Oh, an accident was about to happen! Somebody was in a mad rush to decorate the bonnet of the car with a garland of fresh flowers.

'Fools! Drive faster, Mr Mahapatra. Tell the people it is a punishable offence to block a public road,' Brajeshwar added.

'But these fools have come here from many distant places to express their love and respect for the Maharaja,' Mr Mahapatra argued.

Brajeshwar breathed out a puff of blue smoke and said, 'Once upon a time, they also gathered from many distant places to murder the Maharaja in cold blood. I am not bothered whether they love me or hate me. I cannot resort to playacting with hands joined in silent prayer, bowing respectfully before the public. Drive the car fast, Mr Mahapatra.'

The car blasted its horns in quick succession, sending up clouds of dust behind before disappearing at a turning point.

*

Holding a gun in his hand, Brajeshwar was pacing about in the palace garden.

Some flocks of swans, teals and shelducks were flying noiselessly in the bluish sky. How gloriously was that flock of teals swooping overhead like a garland of jasmine flowers! With perfect aim, Brajeshwar fired the gun. It hit the target and some birds fell onto the ground. His face creased with lines of satisfaction. A gardener rushed to the spot to collect the dead and wounded birds.

Another flock of birds was winging its flight ahead, wildly screaming in the open firmament.

The thirst of their life had not yet been quenched in the Caspian Lake. Hence, over a hundred species of migratory birds fly to the nearby areas of the equator in search of warmth and to escape the severe winter of their native habitat. Their wings had been animated with the call of the remote and their throats with the songs of life. Brajeshwar set his target and fired the gun again. Being hit by the bullets, some of the wounded teal ducks fell to the ground. Beads of blood began to be deposited over their colourful feathers.

Brajeshwar lifted a bird from the ground. The grim reaper of the dead was gradually devouring its brittle body. Brajeshwar threw the bird away in disgust.

Brajeshwar did not like such unproductive dissipation of energy any more. There was no excitement left in murder. So, he began to move towards the palace, reclining his gun over his shoulder with slow steps.

The shadow of the white marble palace was floating midway on the crystalline water of the pool in the garden. Brajeshwar was taken aback by the sudden screeching noise of an unfamiliar bird amidst the grove of cypress bushes.

The palace seemed desolate and bereft of any kind of noise. Brajeshwar was destined to live a solitary, profligate but unrewarding life. Everywhere, he was surrounded by a lustreless plenitude of wealth and resources. With a downward glance, he slowly headed towards the palace.

Some people in the portico were eagerly awaiting the sight of the Maharaja. Hearing the news that Maharaja Ray Brajeshwar Ray had returned to Raj Kanchangarh after a long period, many subjects from many different localities flocked to his palace to meet him. Brajeshwar possessed no state to rule any longer as kingship had been abolished, yet their love and affection for the despotic Maharaja had not reduced even a bit in their subconscious mind. On seeing Brajeshwar, they knelt and bowed their heads before him as a sign of respect. But they hardly merited a sidelong glance from the Maharaja. He handed over the gun to one of his stewards and entered inside straightaway.

Brajeshwar called upon Mr Mahapatra and enquired, 'Why have they gathered here? What do they want? Ask them to leave the place immediately.'

'Huzoor! The way time is changing, it is beneficial to keep them in hand. When they have already arrived over here, won't it be unscrupulous to drive them away?'

'It's natural for time to change. But I am not changed and there is no prospect for change to come over my person in the near future either,' said Brajeshwar in a slightly enraged voice.

Mr Mahapatra went away.

*

Everywhere in the palace, Brajeshwar was greeted with derision by the spotless marble-clad walls. Everything in the palace was smeared with heartless opulence and one could see the multi-hued rose garden through the large casement windows. It seemed as though life had turned out to be the vigourless image of a graceful lady carved in pearl-white marble. It could be felt but could never be relished. Its beauty could be enjoyed but its thirst could never be quenched. Everything about the palace looked bright and spotlessly clean. Here, there were only intense desires and immeasurable bestial powers to satisfy.

Brajeshwar called for his attendant.

An attendant approached the Maharaja and stood near him waiting for his order. Brajeshwar ordered, 'Whisky and soda.'

The attendant arrived with whisky and soda.

Brajeshwar took a sip of the whisky and placed the glass on the table.

'Damodar Rayguru has come to visit you,' said Mr Mahapatra coming closer to the Maharaja.

'Damodar Rayguru?'

'It's the man from Ranidaha who led the mob to gherao your palace during the people's agitation. Let me ask him to leave by saying that it's not possible to meet the Maharaj now,' said Mr Mahapatra.

'Nay, Mr Mahapatra, send him in straight away,' said Brajeshwar.

Damodar Rayguru came in after a few minutes. He had grown quite old. An imprint of oppression was still visible on his bright face, having been part of many agitations and imprisonments throughout his troubled life. Damodar saluted the Maharaja by bowing his head and bending his waist.

'What grievances have you come up with this time, Mr Rayguru? Haven't I fulfilled your sundry demands for long?' asked Brajeshwar.

'Demands? It's rather a regression from poverty to

penury,' Damodar responded wearing a faint smile on his face.

'It's quite normal. Because poverty and penury are the only truths left in this impoverished world. Providence has scribbled nothing on the fate of humankind except futility?'

'What do you mean?'

Brajeshwar lit his pipe and said, 'The meaning is quite clear Mr Rayguru. Oppressing others is an inherent characteristic of humankind. Humankind had founded a state so that they could overcome the oppression perpetrated by people who never hesitate to seize the opportunity of others' weakness and incautiousness to exploit them with both hands. But nobody amongst them had ever apprehended that the state would be more oppressive than the man.'

'Why did we abolish monarchy then?'

Brajeshwar released a puff of smoke from his pipe and said, 'It's because there was a huge drawback in the system of monarchy, Mr Rayguru. I was oppressing and exploiting my subjects without asking for their valuable opinions. But democracy rather relies more upon cruel means of oppression and exploitation in the name of soliciting opinions from the people. Take for instance, in a monarchical set-up, I used to smash you over your head without asking for your approval; according to the statutes of democracy, I must have first procured your consent before smashing your head.'

Brajeshwar let out a burst of huge ringing laughter.

'I, too, gradually started to rely on oppression. Because man believes in nothing but terror. Human society is exclusively built upon the foundation of terror. The societal lives of people will ever remain secure as long as there is the oppressive terror of culture, civilisation, science, wisdom and religion. Without that apprehensive terror, why should a man stay confined within the shackles of society?'

Brajeshwar moved inside the inner room. He had absolutely no time for this kind of nonsense gibberish.

*

It was a time in the evening.

Standing at the casement window of his recreation room, Brajeshwar was fixedly looking at the glittering moonlit garden outside. The silvery moon of the bright night was softly rising above the eucalyptus and casuarina treetops in the distance. The beaker of whisky in Brajeshwar's hand had already finished. Brajeshwar returned from the casement window and sat on a sofa nearby. Several taxidermy tiger heads hunted during different periods were mounted on the lofty walls that looked gigantic, gruesome and terrifying as though the all-devouring angel of death was ready to swallow up all of creation with its fiercely-animated, stuck-out tongue. The hunger of that overpowering force had not yet been satiated. The electric lights surrounding the palace walls were steadily beaming their faint gleam amidst the fiendish stillness of the evening. Brajeshwar pressed the switch of an electric calling bell near him. Nilambar Mahapatra entered after a few minutes. Brajeshwar lighted his pipe and exclaimed, 'What a wonderful evening!'

'Huzoor!'

'But Mr Mahapatra, beauty cannot fully be enjoyed on one's own. Have you made arrangements for that? I mean some young virgin girl . . . unblemished yet!' Brajeshwar exulted, releasing a puff of smoke from his pipe.

'Gone are the days, my lord, when it was easy to abduct any woman you developed a likeness for. Now, it's quite difficult,' said Mr Mahapatra like a man guilty of a heinous crime.

'What difficulty, Mr Mahapatra? Previously, there was the fear of punishment and there was enough power with the administration to capture other's properties by force. And now, we have enough pelf to capture anything we like in exchange for money. I did not believe until recently that money could not buy anything in the world.'

'But can these things be always acquired in exchange for money? And apart from that . . .'

Brajeshwar poured some whisky into the beaker and silently took a few sips. Then, waving the empty beaker before his eyes for a moment, he began to examine something inside and said in a thundering voice, 'I have heard, Mr Mahapatra, that you are in possession of such a precious jewel. You, therefore, need not have to search for it elsewhere.'

Nilambar's sunken eyes began to glitter like two molten fireballs. The lines on his face hardened. He responded in an indignant voice, 'I am dependent on you for my daily bread, sir, but I have not eaten up my conscience yet. I did not believe that anybody on this Earth could ever propose such an offensive thing about a girl before his father.'

Nilambar was about to leave when Brajeshwar called him back, 'Listen, Mr Mahapatra!'

Nilambar paused instantly as if being enthralled by Brajeshwar's commanding voice. Brajeshwar silently paced up and down in the room for some time and then said, 'One cannot manage to live off the wealth of feudalism and sustain the honour and glory of conscience at the same time; you know that very well Mr Mahapatra. Have you ever imagined how many times you have solicited girls from their fathers?'

'I apologise, Huzoor!'

Brajeshwar threw a bunch of keys to Nilambar, pointing towards an iron shelf, and commanded, 'Let the shelf be opened.'

Out of mechanical instinct, Nilambar followed the command and opened the shelf. Piles of costly ornaments were treasured in it. Nilambar's hungry eyes suddenly sparkled at the splendour of gold ornaments.

Brajeshwar continued, 'The queen mother had kept up these precious gold ornaments for the would-be bride of this dynasty. But as you know, Mr Mahapatra, I believe more in forcible possession of things than the easeful attainment of them. Because the things which can be easefully attained are only charitable gifts from others. Hence, you should feel ascertain of the fact that no royal bride in the coming years is going to wear those gold ornaments. Your daughter can have this all if she desires so.'

Hypnotised as if by his words, Nilambar gazed at Brajeshwar's face. 'But I would like to embellish her in my own hands according to my fancy,' Brajeshwar added.

Nilambar felt the ground sinking beneath his feet and unmindfully dropped himself on a nearby couch.

'I am waiting, you should come back soon,' said Brajeshwar and quickly disappeared around the corner.

*

It was a late hour of the night.

The waxing moon of the bright night was gradually setting below the distant treetops. The garden outside the palace was shrouded in the fluid darkness of the night by degrees.

Brajeshwar poured the last few pegs of whisky into the beaker and blurted out, 'Sundari, the beautiful! Nice name! There is no pretence or affectation, it's easy and uncomplicated. You are beautiful indeed, Sundari.'

Sundari was the daughter of Nilambar Mahapatra.

Brajeshwar had learnt her name correctly—Sundari Nirupama.

Sundari stood silently with a downward gaze like an entrapped deer overwrought in frightful amazement. She had no courage left to peer into the inebriated face of Brajeshwar.

'Come closer, Sundari,' said Brajeshwar. 'Why are you still standing there?'

Sundari approached with fearful decisive steps and stood near Brajeshwar.

Brajeshwar lifted the veil from Sundari's forehead and began to pat her chin delicately with his hand. There was a tiny black mole under Sundari's rosy lips. Brajeshwar exclaimed, 'Beautiful! The tiny beauty spot on your chin looks graceful like the secret meeting of a virtuous wife with her prized lover.'

Brajeshwar began to disrobe Sundari with both his hands.

With her unveiled, hesitant demeanour, Sundari looked like a glistening moonlit night in the ruffle.

She was fully naked from below her shoulders.

Brajeshwar stood there with an amused appreciative look on his face as his gaze swept over Sundari's almost nude figure.

Sundari's pair of bright spotless thighs looked like polished marble, crafted as if with great diligence and perseverance by a masterly sculptor.

'Wonderful symmetry!' Brajeshwar exclaimed.

Sundari was hot with shame and covered her face with both of her palms.

Brajeshwar removed all ornaments from her bare body.

The tiny beauty spot under her lips was accidentally smudged by her nimble hand, drawing a black line across her chin as she was trying to protect herself from Brajeshwar's lustful gaze.

Sundari had deliberately painted her chin with a black dot using collyrium from her eyes to enhance the beauty of her face.

'Oh, gosh, but your beauty spot disappeared from your face! There was hardly any necessity of painting a rose with hues.'

Sundari covered her face with her hands out of shame, fear and humiliation and sank on a sofa like the fatigued model of an accomplished sculptor.

Brajeshwar started to pace around the room with his arms crossed on his chest.

'Can you say, Sundari, which one is more beautiful—the lascivious eyes of a man or the bare body of a woman?'

Sundari stared at Brajeshwar in stupefied amazement.

Brajeshwar opened the iron shelf and said, 'All these are yours, Sundari. Take as much as you want, befitting your worth. I must be off now. You can lock the door from inside.'

Brajeshwar hurried into the inner room. Sundari, now fully naked, stood there, fixedly staring at Brajeshwar with a vacant expression. His receding footsteps sounded in the distance and then merged into the weird stillness of the night.

Cigarette

It was the month of Chaitra. The leaves in the trees hummed and feathered as a gentle breeze was blowing through the dense foliage. The moon of the bright fortnight was shining merrily against the vaulted firmament like the bright forehead of a newly-wed young woman, adorned with clear sandalwood paste. Bini's mother alias my wife worriedly tossed her body on the bed.

'When will Suniti return home? The clock has already struck eleven.'

'You know, Bini's mother, you are responsible for your son's erratic behaviour. And who are you seeking an explanation from? How can he return home before finishing the rehearsal and his favourite moonlit walk? What difference can you make by poking your nose into his private business every now and then?'

'Oh! You are reminded of your own bad habits, aren't you?' Bini's mother remarked in a slightly enraged voice.

It was a bright moonlit night of Chaitra. Binita was the eldest daughter of this family. She was married and had a ten-year-old girl child. Navanita was younger to Binita. Her marriage had finished. She had come here for a change in health. Her husband Shushant came to our house yesterday to escort her back home. Sumitra was the youngest daughter in this house. And Suniti was younger than Sumitra. It was he who had been stealing my cigarettes from the case for a few years. Outside, the new moon was shining bright all around. Navanita and her husband had gone on a trip around the town. Circling his arm around Navanita's slender waist, Shushant got inside the taxi. The yellow leaves falling from the trees laid a bed of sweet memories on the untrodden path of brimming youthfulness as Shushant and Navanita wandered around enjoying the beautiful Chaitra evening.

But I have grown old. My beard has turned grey. I often find myself in a bad mood and have developed an irate temperament. 'Do you hear me, Bini's mother or fell asleep?'

'Has he returned yet, Suniti?'

'How many times have I asked you not to enquire about his whereabouts any more? Having a single son does not entail that I should pamper him by lifting him on my shoulders.'

'Look, you shouldn't always throw tantrums at the slightest provocation. It is because of this temper tantrum . . .'

'He is not Suniti that proffers good-mannered behaviour. He should rather be given the name 'Durniti' meaning ill-mannered or corrupted. Badly behaved and a disgrace to the clan! You just do not mention his name before me, Bini's mother. I am totally uninterested.' 'How old have I grown, Bini's mother—sixty, sixty-five or a hundred?'

'Oh, perhaps he is not returning home today! Let him come, wicked boy! I will take him to task tomorrow.'

'Gosh! How come the cigarette case is empty? It's real oppression. A well-planned, systematised oppression! You . . . you can see it for yourself, Bini's mother, what scam is your virtuous son involved with this time? There were ten cigarettes inside the case; I counted them myself. Marcovich branded cigarette—the lone comfort of my old age! This modern etiquette of stealing cigarettes from father's cigarette case should be suitably punished.'

'Why are you blaming my child for nothing? Does Sonu smoke? Have you ever noticed him smoking? He is in his graduation and reaching adulthood. He has his style of enjoying his life. Why should you deprive him of that delight?' Bini's mother returned in an intolerant voice.

I am a 60-year-old man. This Bini's mother, my wife, used to feel terrorised at the slightest negligence in performing her duty at home. How much dread had she nourished in her mind against my person! Of course, I have indeed done much injustice to this virtuous, chaste lady in former times. I have given her many pains. But today, she doesn't even care about me at all. My cigarette case is damn empty. Not a single cigarette left. Ah, Marcovich cigarette! Yet, her careless attitude over the matter is quite obvious.

But the case was not damn empty. Bini's mother passed that to me which still contained a cigarette.

Wow! How beautiful, sublime and intense is this astral Chaitra night! No, no . . . how horrible, unattractive and treacherous is this desolate Chaitra night!

I've dedicated my entire life to a purpose, pouring my youth, energy, and passion into it. However, it seems to have abandoned me, leaving me feeling like an unwanted object. People show no compassion towards me due to my age and weakness. Everywhere I go, I face ridicule and doubt, making me feel like a silly clown in this unfair and harsh world.

'But who is giggling at this late hour of the night? Who chuckled such cheerfully like this moonlight lustre of Chaitra? What is that Bini's mother?'

'How offensive you sound! You're getting old does not entail that the whole world has become old, old man!' Bini's mother screamed out at me.

Oh! Perhaps this soft and sensuous chuckle is coming from Shushant and Navanita's room. Are they laughing at me in derision?

'Let me close the window, Bini's mother. A cold wind is blowing outside. Is there any Veramon tablet left?'

Veramon . . . it's sometimes difficult for me to sleep without taking it.

I have never delivered a speech since I retired from the job of a lecturer. But today, suddenly I was invaded by a desire to deliver a speech. This dozing Bini's mother would serve as the audience and this damn stupid clown of the life-drama would be the speaker!

'What do you think Bini's mother, do I hate Sonu? How could I hate the only male child of the family? Truly speaking, I don't like his attitude and bearing. These young men of today's world do not believe in culture and religion. They tend to react negatively to our rich heritage. Clan carries absolutely no meaning for them.'

The audience, however, is a large-hearted person.

'Please, stop prating like this, or else I will go and sleep in Mita's room. Then you will keep on gossiping with yourself for the entire night.'

Bini's mother left. The elegance of her swaying hips, as she walks, has disappeared for a long time.

Let her go. At this advanced sixty years of age, human beings have no morbid fascination or craze for anything. The only fascination left is Marcovich cigarettes. A mild compliment: 'Sir, your lectures are jaw-droppingly breathtaking! Who can teach Shakespeare more efficiently than you?'

To be or not to be . . .

This century itself is corrupt to the core. It persists without a foundation. It has no heritage, decency or refinement. The things people only value are cheap cigarettes and Hawaiian shirts. Life carries absolutely no meaning for them. Yet, endless competitions ensue and numberless slogans are shouted to accomplish its damn objectives!

Bini's mother hurried back into my room. Mita was busy writing her book, switching on the lights in her room.

'Oh, my God! The house is full of educated oddities that are as efficient as the others. Book writing in midnight hours!'

'Writing love letter instead! The whole night is spent without sleep, to commend the silent tears I never weep!'

'But you're a very saintly person, aren't you? Not for nothing had your father died so prematurely, yelping out at your moral bankruptcy throughout his life. Are you lacking in standards? Never! As the seed, so the plant!'

Bini's mother now easefully drifted into sleep with a calmness of mind. Sometimes she enables herself to sleep like a philosopher.

Huh! We also used to be revolutionists in those fond old days. Haven't we participated in revolutions? But we displayed great moderation on the occasion. No, no . . . it's sheer self-deception! We also used to be wild, harum-scarum youths—unbridled, energetic and undisciplined. But why should they follow in our footsteps? We began to smoke after we passed MA from Presidency College, Calcutta. Sahib Principal! He was a truly saintly man—benign and affectionate. Nowhere will you find a godly person like him in this contemporary world. Also, you won't find such sincere students nowadays. But these fashionable young men of today have savoured the thrill of smoking cigarettes and shouting slogans as early as in their mothers' wombs. But who can excel us in revolutionary zeal? How was I denounced when I set out for Cuttack to appear for the entrance test: 'Nonsense! How can I allow him to go to Cuttack town and study in a British-run school? How disgraceful it is to leave your village and study in town! Let him drop his study.' And didn't we rise and revolt against the decision? Again, how can I forget the day when Mother made the entire house sacrosanct by sprinkling cow dung water on it only because an imported tea set was brought home for the first time from Calcutta? 'Oh! What British utensils have you brought home today? And what red water are you drinking with those cups that look like the water deposited from the thatch eaves? And what leaves are those? You cannot know for sure what untouchable or Muslim people might have touched that thing.' Father bristled in anger at our unorthodoxy. But our unorthodoxy reached the greatest heights when we appointed a Muslim cook at home. Why should we discriminate between people's colour, caste and religion when we knew them all to be equal? And apart from that, Muslim cooks are damn good at cooking dishes like pulao, korma and the like. It was a serious blow to the father's religious beliefs. He promised not to take any food or drink at our home. And he kept his promise till death. Further, a new conflict cropped up in our house when I ultimately notified my father about my desire to marry Krishnamayee. I met her while attending a ceremony in the Brahma Samaj. She was dark-complexioned, doe-eyed and had well-balanced, contoured brows that seemed to conceal all the dark mysteries of the night. Alas, her red quivering lips! However, my marriage, finally, was fixed with Bini's mother.

The clock struck 2 at midnight.

Sonu did not return yet. Wicked boy! Where would have he spent the night today? What would have he eaten? Bini's mother fell asleep. The unclosed window of one room was fiercely beating its head against the wooden frame.

It is Sonu's room.

A-ha! When did he come back and fell asleep? Oh, I see! There must be some secret signals exchanged between the mother and the son. Perhaps, this is the reason why she slipped out of her bed shortly before. How generous and forgiving is a mother's heart! Yet, how petty and selfish it is!

A streak of bright Chaitra moonlight glowed on Sonu's drowsy forehead. How relaxing and lustrous it seems! How lofty is his protruding nasal bridge! I felt as if I was restored to life in his robust body. Nope—I'm not old. I have got a passionate heart that burbles with life. I still possess the strength and confidence of a young man!

I swept my hand delicately on Suniti's drowsy forehead. Long live the new era of youths!

The Chaitra wind howled as it flurried through the leaves and foliage of the trees outside the window. It was gradually getting cold. I pulled a shawl over Suniti's sleeping body for warmth.

But what is that red stain at one corner of his lips? Once upon a time, Krushmamayee also made me feel embarrassed like this. Under that desolate *neem* tree, Krishnamayee kissed me on my lips in the absolute stillness of the night. And my lips were smeared with lipstick stains. Long live this love, this dream and this charmed youthfulness!

The inertness of old age can no longer afflict my youthful mind. There is no drowsiness of Veramon visible in my bright and cheerful face which is but brimming with the surge of eternal youthfulness. It is my new avatar! And she is the new Krishnamayee of my cherished past!

Suniti's Panjabi was hanging on the mosquito curtain. I groped in the pockets for the sheer fun of it. My Marcovich cigarettes! Only two are left. And a folded sheet of paper. Love letter—I suspect!

It carries the lovely flavour of 'Evening in Paris.' It must be a love letter addressed to my son by the new Krishnamayee. I secretly grabbed the letter and tuck it into my waist. And cigarettes? Nay—let them be there. One side of the window slammed shut in the wind. I flung open the window back to its previous position. Let the shimmering moonlight of Chaitra stream in through the open window, and saturate the dreaming bed with its cool, silver lustre.

I shall hide this letter carefully on my shelf.

It will be a total disaster if Bini's mother comes to know about it.

The Guest

Plodding down the dark, deserted alleyway in the middle of the night, Shyamal suddenly hid behind a nearby dustbin. Three police constables walked past him at a distance. The noise of their heavy footsteps pounding along the hard surface sounded eerily in the coagulated gloom of the night.

Shyamal cowered in fear as they passed near him at arm's length. Had they encountered him at this late hour of the night, they would have dumped him in the lock-up for the whole night. Soggy ground, stench of urine and mosquito bites! A living hell! A burning example of how people's government can reduce itself to an uncivilised, barbaric and oppressive mechanism by hurling humans into this living hell in the name of maintaining peace and justice in society.

The government had issued an order to restrict Shyamal's freedom of movement. He was declared an enemy of the country because he rebelled against the government. But is the country analogous to the government? God knows!

A clock in the nearby house struck midnight. It was getting very late tonight.

Shyamal was returning from a secret meeting of the 'Death Squad'. The meeting was held in a collapsed, abandoned building at the end of this dark alleyway. Nobody could say when this two-story building was constructed. Long ago, a family was living in that house all of whom died prematurely of tuberculosis. Nobody in the localities ever dared to set foot on this cursed land. The area inside the house was uninhabitable, with dense overgrowth of bushes and plants. The meeting was held in that secret place.

The door was locked from the inside. Shyamal knocked softly at the door like a criminal. The house was damn silent like the land of the dead. It's quite probable that the elder brother had not slept yet. He must be busy examining the documents of his clients now. Usually, he went to bed at late hours of the night. A certain inertness crept over his entire body as he meditated on the consequences of being exposed before his brother. He was left with no courage to confront the strong reprimands of his brother at this advanced hour of the night. Again, you cannot raise a protest against one you depend on for your daily bread.

But Mother was awake. On this freezing, cold night she must be lying desultorily on the bed with an open ear.

Shyamal was right. Mother was not asleep yet. She opened the door for Shyamal to come in.

'Mother! O mother!'—Shyamal only recited the word inwardly for hundred times.

Shyamal quietly tiptoed into his small room down the courtyard. Nirmala too was not asleep yet. Her feet were shaking under the blanket.

'Nima,' Shyamal called.

There was no response. A dish of curry and a plate of dry chapattis were set out on a tiny table next to her head. They might have got frozen by the cold. Oh, if Nirmala could serve him a cup of hot coffee!

'Nima,' Shyamal called again. His voice resembled that of a criminal.

Like a wounded serpent, Nirmala yelled out at him from under the blanket, 'Where were you roaming around at this midnight hour? Why do you inflict such systematic tortures on me?'

Shyamal was ready for the explosion.

Taking off his shirt, he calmly replied, 'There were so many works to perform. You cannot understand. Hence, try to sleep silently.'

Shyamal's nonchalant behaviour infuriated his wife to a great extent.

'That sounds a pretty good deal, huh?' she scoffed. 'That's why you have to beg for food from others for the sustenance of your family.'

Shyamal had no patience for these useless arguments and altercations. Lifting the plate off the table, he sat on the floor to eat.

Nirmala dragged herself out of the bed to snatch the plate containing chapatti and curry, spurned it to one corner of the room with a quick hand and said in a tearful voice, 'No, you cannot eat this animal food before me. Why should you feed yourself with dry chapattis and stale curry when other members of the family are served different types of fresh food items?'

'Yet how many among the society are fortunate enough to have this dry chapattis and stale curry?' Shyamal replied unexcitedly.

Then he contentedly glugged a glass of water and lifted himself from the ground. The clock in the elder brother's room struck 1 at midnight. Burying her face in the pillow, Nirmala burst into tears and said in a snivelling voice, 'Why did you get married then? You can let your life go waste like this but it is absurd to play with the lives of others. Aren't you ashamed of yourself?'

'What do you want me to do?' Shyamal asked with a marked irritation in his voice.

'You should precisely mend your ways and learn how to earn your living as other members of the society do,' said Nirmala. 'How long will you manage your family by begging before others?'

'It's impossible on my part to conduct myself the way others do, you know that well,' said Shyamal.

'Why did you marry me then?' Nirmala roared.

'After all, I am never married to you,' Shyamal argued. 'Marriage of the bodies or marriage of the minds as narrated in cheap novels is not marriage, Nirmala, in the true sense of the words. It's but a socially sanctioned means to satisfy the inflamed desires of the restless youthfulness. But the ideal marriage is the real one. And I'm never married to you in that sense. You can be my wife, but not my partner. I can never give the honour to a wife which a partner deserves.'

'How mean and spiteful you sound,' Nirmala cried out in protest.

Shyamal put on his shirt and stormed out of the house.

Shyamal's elder brother had fallen asleep but his mother was still snoozing in the bed. Shyamal stealthily opened the door lest they should be awakened by the noise and quickly snuck back down the road.

'Mother! O, mother!' The house burst into loud wails of pain behind like a helpless child.

It was a cloudless, starry night. The highway looked desolate and bereft of any kind of noise.

Shyamal hurriedly moved towards the station. He was convicted of treason and declared an enemy to his friends and relatives. Forsaken and banished from human society!

A small, modest railway station.

The first light of the dawn rose over the eastern horizon. The coconut fronds, under the cover of freezing fog, glittered in the morning sunshine. The sheaves of ripened paddy on either side of the road bowed their heads under the weight of the fresh dews of the night. The fragrance of dews and ripened paddies filled the cool air of the morning.

The path ahead descended steeply to a pretty little village called Nayanpur. The dunes formed in the middle of the empty-bellied River Birupa, on the other side of the village, were now visible at a distance. It was a hotbed of malaria, flood, drought and abject penury. Shyamal had been to this village last year on the occasion of defending the cause of the common villagers who were planning to launch an agitation against the imposition of certain taxes which they thought to be illegal.

Shyamal soon came within the hailing distance of the villagers. Some nude, filthy children were rushing towards him, exposing their bare bodies in the biting cold. The delicate sunshine of the early morning was pleasant to their bare skin.

They recognised Shyamal from a distance and screamed out, 'Hey, look, Babu! Babu!'

Soon they gathered around Shyamal, beaming their curious faces, as if to welcome the most wanted and awaited guest to their village on this beautiful morning. Endless affection swam across their querying eyes and unflagging bliss filled their searching souls.

Shyamal's eyes became moist with tears, seeing the derelict condition of these bemused observers.

'Arey! How are you all?' Shyamal queried.

There ensued a contest among the children as to who would reply first. All of them said in unison, regretfully, 'We are not going to school any more, Babu. Our school has been closed. The teacher went to Calcutta to work in a jute factory. Nobody paid him the salary over here.'

The school was established as a result of Shyamal's enthusiasm and endeavour.

Shyamal reached the end of the village. The sun-tanned, dilapidated temple of Lord Mahadev was now visible to him. The champak flowers in the tree by the temple wall outnumbered the leaves.

Shyamal was now walking along the public road of the village. The procession of the nude village boys was still following him at a distance as though to celebrate the victory of a recently fought battle.

At first, Shyamal came across Jagu Swain's hut. Sitting on his outer veranda and exposing his bare back, the old man Jagu was basking under the glory of the morning sun. Seeing a shadow approaching him, he turned aside and found Shyamal standing near him.

'How are you, Uncle Jagu?' Shyamal greeted.

'Gosh, what an auspicious day is today!' Jagu chirruped, invaded by a plethora of delightful feelings. 'I didn't believe that you would set foot in this village again. Do not ask about our condition, Babu. We know we have to survive against all odds, accepting our lot in this deserted village. Nobody in the world seems to be concerned about us. Several times, the villagers have insisted to post a letter to you, regarding our cause. We are not fortunate enough to get a drop of kerosene to light our lamp-wick in the evening and our foods are all infested with insects. We are even deprived of a piece of cloth to cover our bodies. Again, we have to go from door to door, begging for preventive potions at the time of disease. And where from we get the money to send a letter by post?'

In no time, the entire village began to gather around Shyamal. Their eyes glowed with the delight and the mirth of welcoming their favourite guest.

Last time, Shyamal stayed for a month in Jagu's hut. He would also stay there now.

'Arey, this time we are not going to bid him goodbye so early!' Jagu blurted. 'He will stay with us at least for a month. Please do come in, my child, and wash yourself with water.'

Jagu escorted Shyamal to his hut. Standing in one corner, the nude boys, who were the precursor of this unexpected delight, were observing Shyamal with utmost curiosity and amazement. Yet nobody spared a word of thanks to them.

Jagu's youngest son appeared, carrying a pot of water and a piece of teeth cleaning twig, and placed them on the floor. Shyamal enabled himself to wash his face. Oh, how refreshing is the water! How soothing! Shyamal was inwardly musing as to how strange his relationship with these oppressed, browbeaten destitute—the unconditional lifters of the civilisation's sundry burdens. He felt like a native of this tiny village called Nayanpur. As if he had become the most favourite person in the eyes of each and every resident of the village—a worthy son of the soil!

The old man Jagu had sown some mustard seeds on the seedbed situated in his backyard. The delicate fragrance, emanating from the numberless yellow mustard blooms, began to fill the gentle breeze of the morning.

That a vast, boundless world lay sprawl outside this cramped little house was being realised by Shyamal by degrees. How insignificant is the conventional love and affection of this mundane world before the eternal tenderness of this enormous world!

Once you collapse a house, the doors of thousand houses shall be opened to welcome you in.

Jagu called his youngest son immediately inside the hut and said, 'Rush to Kusuna Sahu's teashop across the river and quickly bring some tea leaf and sugar. Tell him that father has earnestly requested a *chittak* of sugar. He will deliver a packet of *moong* to your house as soon as it is harvested. A distinguished guest, hailed from some distant village, has visited our house today.'

Bread and Moon

The textile mill workers' general strike against capitalists had been continuing for a month.

The strike had gathered momentum and was gradually consolidating power, irrespective of the fiendish stratagem of the rivalling union, the vain attempts of the mill owners to foil the protest and above all, against all pressures from various government mechanisms.

The leadership and prudence of the local communist leader were commendable.

After moving door-to-door on the workers' street to canvas and encourage the mill workers, collecting subscription fees from them and mobilising the workers into a protest march around the city, shouting the slogan 'Red Flag Zindabad', comrade Binod felt utterly powerless to work further. Returning exhausted from there, he lay sprawled on the piles of pamphlets and newspapers in the corner of a small room of the party office. As soon as he went to bed, he drifted off into a deep sleep.

A few moments later, comrade Lalita entered the room. She had a slender and flexible body coupled with a small waist. She was a good writer and a woman of few words. Her job was to explicate all English circulars and booklets in exquisite detail. She also bore the responsibility of publishing the weekly newsletters. With the launch of the general strike, another important task had also been assigned to her—the task of writing the party bulletin.

It was comrade Lalita's office room. She switched on the lights. Adjacent to the open window in the west was a small table. Papers, books and newspapers lay scattered all over the table in a mess. Three framed photographs of similar size with Marx in the middle hung from the wall. Left to Marx was Stalin and on the right was Lenin.

A rusty calling bell from the olden days lay in the piling mess of papers over the table. Lalita pressed that bell thrice with her forefinger.

The office help named Ramu hurried into the room. He too was a comrade—the son of a common worker.

'Coffee,' said Lalita.

Ramu went away.

Outside, the new moon was shining bright all around.

The party office was situated towards the end of the factory area.

A red gravel road went around in a tight curve outside the window. Occasionally, a bullock cart or a passer-by moved along the rugged road. A rocky terrain sprawled across it along several miles of the boundless wasteland, touching the dim verge of the horizon.

The calmness of the night was enraptured with the intoxicating fragrance of an unfamiliar flower.

Lalita switched off the lights in the room, overcome with a lethargic weariness and perplexity.

A streak of bright moonlight, streaming through the

open window, illuminated Lalita's lap. Every corner of her heart became instantly bright and cheerful with ineffable completeness and satiety. She mused for a moment. She thought about how through the pages of human history, many struggles and revolutions had gone futile and become extinct in the process of arguments and altercations. Yet this fine moonlit evening seemed eternally graceful. There was no end to its conduction of delight.

Lalita switched on the lights again. Alas, these escapist, counter-revolutionary bourgeois values and their formal concept of beauty!

Comrade Binod's faint snore was gradually getting abnormally noisy.

Lalita had not yet realised that Binod was sleeping peacefully near her. She was taken aback by the sudden sound of the snore and glanced at Binod. He was clad in a pair of dirty trousers and a shirt and wore a pair of Kabuli sandals that were torn. His half-sleeved shirt bore a party badge on the left side of his shoulders in the design of a sickle and a hammer.

Ramu returned with a cup of coffee. Lalita asked him to bring another cup of coffee and he went away.

Lalita inwardly praised comrade Binod for his leadership and Marxist scholarship. On any occasion, Binod could talk about Marxist philosophy for hours without interruption. Binod once fell in love with a girl. His passion for the girl was also duly reciprocated. Their marriage was almost finalised in accordance with the tradition of *Gandharva* marriage, which is based on free choice and mutual attraction. But the father of the girl turned out to be an haute bourgeoisie. Upon hearing his daughter's choice, he clarified before both of them that it was not objectionable to him even if the groom chose to wear *tilak* on his forehead as suggested by the mystic saint, Sri Chaitanya of Nadia, but wearing the badge of sickle and hammer was just unacceptable.

Binod came back extremely disappointed. However, his disappointment was not caused by the futility of love. Had a girl like Leela joined the party, it would provide a further boost to the growth and spread of communism. Yet, Binod never neglected to send Leela a copy of the party bulletin regularly. When some of his friends began to poke fun at his futile love, he confronted them by saying, 'Marx has said, "Nothing is being, everything is becoming" meaning nothing in the world is fixed or motionless which entails that love is never divested of movement. There is nothing to worry about if love has a movement towards futility in the dialectics of love-making.'

Ramu entered the room with another cup of coffee.

Overcome with a youthful fickleness of the mind, Lalita stealthily moved from her chair over to where Binod was asleep and tapped his forehead with her delicate fingers.

Binod rubbed his sleepy eyes and sluggishly sat on the piles of old newspapers.

'Would you like to have a cup of coffee, comrade?' asked Lalita.

Binod's eyes sparkled and his face glowed with the pleasure and satisfaction of the unexpected.

'Thanks, comrade!' said Binod.

They sat down at the table, quietly sipping their coffee.

The landscape outside glittered under the bright moonlight. The boundless wasteland was shimmering softly, clad in the silvery silence of the night.

Somewhere from the stony upland outside the window, a cheerful and soporific note of the raga Nageshwar from a flute began to ripple through the cool air of the night.

'Has the bulletin for tomorrow been sent to the press, comrade Lalita?' enquired Binod.

Lalita was inwardly reflecting on the lines of a romantic poem, 'O doting moon, the encumbrances of thousand miles betwixt thou and I are squeezed, thou hast descended my charmed casement, veiled as a lover in a secret meeting. O admirable! Absolute sweetheart! Bury me deeper in your warm embrace.'

'Arrangements are being made to organise a large assembly of the mill workers tomorrow evening,' said Binod. 'The other mill workers from the industrial area have also given their consent to join us from tomorrow. The bulletin that has to be prepared by you, therefore, needs to be as sharp as a bullet. It would be great to compose a song for the occasion to be recited at the beginning of the assembly as a chorus.'

'Of what kind?' asked Lalita amusingly.

'Anything like this one will do,' said Binod.

We produced golden crops

On barren and infertile soils

By the sweat of our brows …

Lalita let out a huge, satirical laughter.

Feeling awkward and ill at ease, Binod asked in an embarrassing voice, 'But what makes you laugh?'

'Nothing,' said Lalita casually.

Binod groped around in his pocket, pulled out a cigarette and lit it.

Pervaded by a languorous weariness, Lalita peered at the photograph of Marx hanging on the wall in rapt attention. 'Oh, down with this Marxist philosophy! Your work, *Economical Interpretation of History*, has made man a greedy pig, life for whom has simply reduced to a question of subsistence. The ultimate aim of human life in your interpretation is only to eat a stomachful of food. You have rendered the bread more tempting than the moon in the eyes of men. Plentiful production has become your sole objective in life. But that, there's still some higher goal to achieve, you have not provided any clue about that fact.'

Binod flicked the glowing cigarette butt through the window and said in a grave voice, 'It has come to my notice that since a few days, you have grown rather escapist, comrade. Freud has termed this kind of escapism as death instinct. In Buddhist philosophy, it is called 'Abhidhamma' or ultimate reality. The instinctual craving of mankind to be merged with the cosmic void is but the downright weakness of the mind—a bourgeois lavishness and a spiritual dormancy; in the words of Erich Fromm, it is a form of negative liberty.'

Lalita internally felt irritated by Binod's grandiloquent talks. She could not tolerate bookworms of this kind at all, who did not have any self-identity or personal freedom. What Marx had said, what Freud's opinion about a certain thing was, what Fromm had written about and where; as if they were the only and ultimate facts of human life on earth. And what emerged out of these dry speculations were but sheer foolishness, mental weakness and bourgeois lavishness.

'I have heard a lot about that, comrade,' said Lalita.

'Let's go outside for a walk instead. It's a wonderful moonlit night.'

Had it been any other day, Binod would have turned

down her proposal, calling it counter-revolutionary bourgeois lavishness and started to explain the esoteric titbits of Lenin's insurrection tactics or conspiratorial revolt. But today, after the labour and fatigue of the whole day, he was desperately craving the coolness and calmness of the moonlit night.

'Let's go then,' said Binod.

During their walk, they traversed a long way down the vast wasteland. Now they could not even see the tall buildings of the city they had left behind any more. Everywhere the land was surrounded by the encompassing sprawl of the rocky terrain, steadily spreading out in all directions and the capricious fickleness of the silvery moonbeams.

Binod and Lalita perched atop a raised slope on the stony surface. Ideas on what Marx had said to Engels were occasionally exploding along Binod's fiery tongue like the popping of popcorn in a heated frying pan.

'Well, didn't Marx say anything about this moonlit night somewhere?' queried Lalita, rather humorously.

Binod was inwardly devising an appropriate response to the query when a wooden flute weaved in its soulful melody, cascading from the distant ocean of the sparkling moonlight. The mellifluous note of the flute seemed to be perfectly intertwined with the uneven, rocky terrain, the calm and still night, and the dappled fickleness of the moonlight lustre. Lalita and Binod were held spellbound by the melodious music that floated through the thick, nocturnal air.

After a few minutes, two shadowy figures came along and sat at a place a little away from them. The soft melody of the flute continued to reverberate along the landscape without pause. As if the fountain of life, cutting a deep chasm through the stony crest, longed to be united with the ocean of moonlight.

Binod and Lalita were filled with an irrepressible inquisitiveness to observe the duo.

They lifted themselves from their perches.

The trilling music of the flute stopped as they approached them.

Lalita and Binod came closer to them and recognised the duo as Nayana and Kaajari. They were the workers of the same mill where the strike was launched. Originally, they hailed from the Chota Nagpur Division in eastern India.

They were unable to earn their wages as a result of the strike. They possibly had to spend the night on empty stomachs. Still, they felt complete with the plenitude of life's bounties.

'You can play the flute wonderfully, can't you Nayana?' asked Lalita.

'Yes, sister,' Nayana replied in a Chhattisgarhi accent. 'We love to wander around forests and hills like this when a bright moon rises above our land.'

It was late in the night. Lalita and Binod were again returning to the party office.

Lalita was introspecting, 'Here lie the pitfalls of Marxism. Life cannot simply be reduced to a formula of production and distribution. Handsome wages and stomachfuls of food can be a necessity of life, but not its sole objective. Who are these luxuriant showers of moonlight and nature's bounties meant for then? Life is much more beautiful than mere existence. Engrossed in its uproarious struggles, Marxism has become oblivious of the beauty and charm of life.'

'How content both of them looked!' exclaimed Lalita.

Binod gasped at Lalita. In some constricted corner of his heart, an appalling voice revolted in dismay. It was hurting softly but painfully on his tender heart. Nayana's flute resounded again, piercing through the eerie stillness of the night. The gentle breeze seemed to hold the fragrance of the *henna* flower adorning Kaajari's locks of hair.

Binod lifted his eyes from the ground and glanced at Lalita.

He was struck motionless by the overwhelming beauty of Lalita's slender and graceful body, bathed in the faint shimmer of overflowing moonlight. But the next moment, Binod reasoned out this infatuation as sheer bourgeois emotionalism.

Lalita and Binod were returning to the party office through a pathway on the rocky terrain.

They could now see the party office in the distance.

On returning, Lalita again had to engage herself in preparing the party bulletin. Her body and mind grew intoxicated with tiredness and perplexity.

The soft, indistinct tune from Nayana's flute was still resonating around the landscape amidst the tranquillity and loneliness of the moonlit night.

Lalita realised as though the bright, ever-charming life, that nature has to offer amid a thousand uproarious struggles for existence, was but a fierce onslaught against the insufficiency, bleakness and conflictual tendencies embodied in the theory and praxis of Marxism.

The Female Dancer

It was time for the evening aarti at the temple of Lord Kruttibasa. The entire temple reverberated with the sounds of the flute, lyre, mridang, gongs and cymbals. Yayati Keshari, the Emperor of Utkal, was seated silently before the Linga, eyes closed in deep meditation. Many respectable feudal lords and councillors of the King's Court sat around him in meditative postures. Brajanath, the chief priest of the temple, was performing the aarti, waving the holy lamps before the idol while chanting sacred hymns in praise of the deity. Devadasi Purnima swayed from side to side in a circle to the song's pounding rhythm in the courtyard of the entrance hall. Purnima's waist, thighs, breasts and arms became animated with youthful exuberance and devotional self-surrender at the feet of the deity.

The young sculptor, Natawar, stood at one corner of the entrance hall. He seemed like an amiable young man. Many artists and sculptors had arrived from across Utkal to complete the construction of the Kruttibasa temple. Natawar was one among them. He was a stunningly handsome man with a sturdy, well-proportioned body. He was clad in red-ochre clothes and wore a blue scarf around his waist. Silver bracelets adorned both his swarthy arms. Hanging on his muscular chest were some curled gold necklaces and from his ears hung a pair of long earrings. He possessed long hair that brushed against his shoulders. He gazed with wonder and awe at the sportively charming gesticulations of Devadasi Purnima as she danced to the hypnotic rhythm of the music.

Suddenly, there was a break in Purnima's complex dance pattern. She fixedly glanced at Natawar, overwhelmed with excitement and emotion. The chief priest squinted his angry, reddened eyes at Purnima. Yayati Keshari still sat there in quiet meditation. Perhaps, he had not noticed Purnima's breach of cadence yet. But the chief priest's vexed, askance look at once energised her inert body. Responding to the beautiful rhythm of the music, her feet became animated once again with complex dance steps. She resumed her frenzied dancing and ultimately fainted before the idol of Lord Kruttibasa. Her delicate, dancing body quivered like a reptile and tears rolled down her lovely cheeks. The stone idol of Lord Lingaraja possibly failed to grasp the depth of her appealing tears; neither did the chief priest penetrate the worth of her warm tears, but Purnima understood their true significance.

O Lord Lingaraja! Do grant us forgiveness if the attraction of hearts is deemed to be a sin!

The aarti was about to end. Yayati Keshari returned from the temple, escorted by the feudal lords and councillors of the King's Court. The chief priest closed the main door of the temple. But Purnima still lay on the floor of the courtyard with downcast eyes. Her body faintly glinted in the pale moonlight which was streaming through the railings of the courtyard. The chief priest approached her and called out, 'Purnima!'

Perhaps she did not hear him, so he called out once more. 'Purnima!'

Purnima lifted her eyes from the ground and glanced

at the chief priest. Her large, gentle eyes which were painted with vermilion streaks soon became moist with warm tears.

Purnima stood up, her heart hammering inside her brittle body. She looked even more pitiable bathed in the lustrous moonlight.

'You have sinned, Purnima,' said the chief priest. 'Unforgivable in the eyes of God.'

'Sin!' Purnima gaped.

'Yes, you have sinned against God,' said the chief priest. 'You have dedicated your life as a devadasi to Lord Lingaraja. This weakness in your character is a terrible sin.'

'But I am also a woman and possess a woman's heart,' Purnima responded.

'Do not argue,' said the priest. 'The youthful exuberance in your emotional bearing and the tenderness which you have developed for Natawar are unforgivable crimes.'

'Do forgive my ignorance of the scriptures, priest,' Purnima said at length. 'But if the fragrance of the flower resists governance by the petals, then who is to blame for the breach—the fragrance or the petals? The blame lies with the person who has infused the flowers with such an intoxicating fragrance.'

'I would prefer not to hear the adjudication of vice and virtue from the mouth of a devadasi,' said the chief priest. 'If you have faith in Lord Lingaraja, and if you believe in the doctrine of vice and virtue, you must perform penance to atone for the sin.'

'Tell me, priest, how am I supposed to atone for the sin?' Purnima said in a subdued, tearful voice. 'I am an ignorant lady. Please suggest to me the way of deliverance from this sin.'

'You should behave sensibly, and get over your sudden infatuation with Natawar,' said the chief priest. 'Can you do it, Purnima?'

Purnima quietly looked up at the evening sky and saw a pale full moon visible behind a patch of clouds. It was almost as if she was searching for an answer to the question in the faint moonlight.

She did not know if her fascination for Natawar was morally culpable or if in fact, it was a blind infatuation or a mere illusion. Yet, she believed that her passion for Natawar was as pious and untainted as the first light of dawn. As sincere and forthright as God's beautiful creation. In Natawar's fascinated eyes, she had discovered the history of her previous lives. As if the relationship between their hearts was intimate and had an inseparability established quite long ago. The moral judgment between right and wrong could not slacken that bond, nor could the fear of transgression defile those genuine sentiments. Nothing could break the connection which like a vine grew into their passionate hearts.

Purnima began to walk with slow, tentative steps and came out of the entrance hall. Some exquisite flower petals fell from her loosening locks of hair. The chief priest stood there in the cloud-bedimmed moonlight like an immovable stone figure. Under the strict discipline of Brahmacharya, his spirited youthfulness met an early death. In his youthful, unruffled life of self-restraint, he had sometimes suffered the pangs of passion; but it was suppressed by the pressure of the judgment between right and wrong, virtue and vice. Not on a single day in his life had he given free rein to these frailties of the mind. Now of course that tameless, irresistible spirit of youth had been exhausted. He had relentlessly dedicated his entire life to the service of Lord Lingaraja, practising ascetic austerity. Yet, even today, at some points, he was still confronted with the unresolved question of that neglected youth— was this eternal attraction of hearts a sin? But today, in the serene moonlight, he felt as though he had issued an unjust command to Purnima. Believing this unresolved, incomplete truth, he had ruthlessly murdered his turbulent youth. And now, he was going to murder Purnima's brimming youthfulness which had been nourished and ennobled by the primitive instincts of God's creation. Suddenly, it dawned on him that if heaven was real, then the world was even more so. Accordingly, there was no sense in ignoring the actual human world for the sake of God's ideal heaven.

The desolate evening, the dappled temple premises, the pale moonlit sky, the faint twittering of the slumbering dove couple sheltering in some warm corner of the nest amidst the dense foliage—in the grey eyes of the chief priest— all transformed at once into a beautiful, blessed world which seemed even more sublime and graceful than an imaginary heaven. Every object in this mortal, mundane world; including its frailties, sins, injustices, attraction, infatuation and joy is all beautiful and fascinating. The restful slumber of that dove couple in a corner branch of that Ashoka tree may be deemed as sinful and elusive, yet that illusion appeared more sacred and magnificent than the golden flowers of Parijata which grow in that shadowy heaven.

He had imposed an unjust decision on Purnima. Following his pointless precepts and misleading philosophy, Purnima might erase all traces of her blossoming tenderness for Natawar from her heart. The pangs of futility might destroy the lives of two young lovers. He felt like going back to Purnima once again to announce the irrelevance of his worthless advice. 'Nay, Purnima, I have given you the wrong advice. The emotional exuberance of youth is not a sin. The attraction between two faithful hearts beating in unison is not a crime. It is sacred and pristine. You should go back to Natawar, Purnima!'

But the next moment, he felt that there was nothing to feel desperate about when one had dedicated her youthful life to the service of Lord Lingaraja. It was too worthy a feeling to be deviated by instinctual concerns. He had given Purnima the right advice!

*

The night rolled in.

Sleep eluded Purnima's moist eyes. Some streaks of faint moonlight illuminated her sleepless, solitary bed. A couple of birds, perched on the branches of a nearby tree, twittered merrily under the moonlit sky, their songs filling the air with brilliant melody.

Natawar appeared outside Purnima's casement window. Immaculately groomed for the secret meeting, he looked even more handsome than ever.

'You have come, Natawar,' said Purnima in a tearful, whispering voice, etched with emotion and excitement.

'Yes, Purnima! You had signalled me to come up, hadn't you?'

'No, do go back, Natawar, I have committed a mistake in the spur of the moment. It is a sin.'

'Well! I shall go back, Purnima,' said Natawar. 'Beauty has always betrayed me as much as it has fascinated me. I, therefore, prefer to stay away from the beautiful. Also, I am not ignorant of the fact that the dream which I nourished in my heart will be greeted with derision and disbelief. Yet, I would like to know what makes you deem it a sin. It's not sensible to deem it a sin when the odour of the rose likes to merge with the open air, the meandering current of the river wishes to dissolve into the ocean's breast, the golden light of dawn exposes the lotus veil, and the primitive prakriti sends signals of its union with the primordial Purusha.'

'Do go back, Natawar,' Purnima implored, resting her chin on the casement window, and allowing her tears to roll down her cheeks. 'I understand everything. But I respect the command issued by the chief priest: "No Purnima, you have dedicated your life as a devadasi to the service of Lord Lingaraja. This frailty in your character is a sin".'

'It's unscrupulous to confound emotions with frailties,' Natawar said, quite unperturbed.

'I do not understand the holy scriptures, Natawar,' said Purnima.

'Well, I am leaving, Purnima,' said Natawar. 'May God grant you strength to remain unshaken in your commitment. But let me tell you that it does not make sense to ignore human feelings for the sake of the divine. How could you show such callous disregard for human relationships? You are blinded by your faith.'

Natawar gradually merged into the mess of leaves and foliage of the distant Ashoka tree. Purnima cried, 'Wait, Natawar! Do not go away.'

Natawar turned around and fixed his penetrating gaze on Purnima. The entire place looked pale and phantasmal under a rosy, twilit sky. Purnima rushed out to him and clutched his hands, 'Do not leave me Natawar! I can take the risk of committing that sin. I do not want to enter God's paradise or gain his eternal grace any more. I am essentially a woman with my sudden fears, irrational whims, instinctive worries and that fine sensibility. Do lock me in your warm embrace, Natawar!'

'Your lifelong dedication and perseverance will be spoiled in an instant by this momentary weakness of the mind,' said Natawar. 'How can you forget the command of the priest?'

'Are you scoffing at my helplessness?' Purnima queried as she pressed her face against his chest.

The teardrops trickling from her sullen eyes dazzled in the lustre of the faint moonlight.

'Life in the present world has become remarkably complicated, Purnima,' said Natawar, as he put his hand under her chin and lifted her face to his. 'Man has forgotten the world in the hope of gaining paradise, neglected human relationships in the course of justifying his connection to God and overlooked the beauty and charm of life as he is engaged in the relentless pursuit of ideals. Why should man crave paradise if futility, anguish and barrenness deliberately plunder the happiness of human life? This eternal union between a man and a woman is not a sin, Purnima. This primaeval attraction of souls, which brings into existence this beautiful, benign world, the glorious sky, the deep blue sea, and many more beautiful things, cannot be a crime.'

'I know, Natawar,' said Purnima.

The bed of grass beneath the grand and enormous sky became saturated with evening dew. Purnima was fast asleep, resting peacefully on Natawar's lap. The dawn was yet to break. The pole star was shining merrily against the eastern sky. The faint lights of the distant stars glowed against Purnima's marble forehead. 'You should leave now, Purnima,' said Natawar. 'The dawn is about to break.'

A violent thunderstorm was raging in the deep recesses of Purnima's subconscious mind. She was faced with the dilemma of choosing between God and man. Purnima did not know who emerged victorious in this dragged-out battle between God and man. But she knew for certain that in this eternal, uncertain struggle between virtue and vice, she had turned out to be the vanquished. The chief priest's angry, reddened eyes flashed through Purnima's depressed mind: "Death is not the opposite of life, but a part of it. There is a life after death where one has to appear for the ultimate judgement of all the virtues and vices of one's previous life." She then conjured up the image of a furious Lord Lingaraja, descending with his fatal trident from heaven. The sharp ends of the trident stabbed her through her delicate breast. The next moment, the wearied, serene figure of Natawar began to float around in her mind. Purnima regained all her lost confidence and mental tranquillity seeing those engrossed eyes of Natawar. "Do not be worried, Purnima. It's not a sin to be alive to the beauty and charm of life." Suddenly, the chief priest's moral admonition began to resonate in her sensitive ears like a clap of thunder: "Death is not an end to life on earth, Purnima. Do not forget that you have dedicated your life as a devadasi to Lord Lingaraja. Will you dare to offer this profane, violated youth in the holy shrine of Lord Lingaraja tomorrow morning? You will be severely punished, Purnima, with divine retribution."

'I want nothing less than death, Natawar,' Purnima blurted out, caught up in a maelstrom of conflicting emotions, abruptly lifting herself from Natawar's lap. 'Life has become intolerable for me.'

'What bothers you, Purnima?' asked Natawar. There was a marked amazement in his voice.

'I have committed an unforgivable sin against God, Natawar,' said Purnima weeping hot tears. 'I cannot penetrate your just arguments, but I am one of the devadasis of Lord Lingaraja. His holy shrine will be desecrated by my stained soul.'

'Purnima!' said Natawar apologetically, and gave her an entreating look.

Purnima held her diamond-studded ring close to her lips and said, 'Farewell Natawar! Adieu, dearest! This is our final union in this life. But it is my prayer to that Lord Lingaraja whom I have dedicated my entire life that if there is a rebirth, do allow me to be born into the uncomplicated life of the animal world! Let my life not be deprived of the charm and ease of living because of the judgemental decisions between virtue and vice!'

Purnima's cold, powerless body tumbled down the bed of grass.

*

One day, Emperor Yayati Keshari went forth to inspect the incomplete Lingaraja temple, accompanied by his retinue of ministers and other officers of the King's Court. The chief priest, Brajanath, escorted him to the temple. Suddenly, Yayati Keshari paused at a certain place. A startlingly lifelike image of a female dancer performing complex dance steps was chiselled to perfection on a lifeless rock. Her locks of hair were adorned with bunches of beautiful flowers, her elongated neck swayed to the rhythm of the music, the well-formed, entwining arms looked as tender as evergreen creepers, her uncovered lotus bud-like breasts bounced up as a result of her dancing movements, a girdle set with circular bits embellished her slender waist above her round thighs that looked like the trunks of a plantain tree, protruding along the fanciful clothing, and tinkling anklets, set with emerald, enriched her nimble feet. Yayati Keshari, suitably awestruck, could only stare in wonder. At a place, not far from him, stood Natawar, his eyes fixed unblinkingly on the stone figure of that female dancer.

'This is infallibly the image of Devadasi Purnima!' exclaimed Yayati Keshari. 'Who's its sculptor?'

Natawar saluted the Maharaja and silently stood before him with downcast eyes.

'The entire image smacks of lustfulness, intemperance and immorality,' said the Maharaja. 'Under whose instructions did you dare to model that image?'

'The image which at once struck the Maharaja with wonder and awe, that imperishable beauty cannot be an offshoot of immorality, Huzoor,' Natawar replied unperturbedly.

'Dislodge the image immediately from the compound wall of the temple,' the Maharaja ordered his guards. 'Better if it is destroyed. How inappropriate it is to build that statue on the sacred temple wall that embodies desire and lustfulness! How long has this wickedness been concealed from my sight, sculptor?'

Suddenly, the chief priest spoke out, 'Do revoke your order, Maharaja, I pray to you!'

'What are you saying, priest?' enquired the Maharaja. 'It's amazing how you can be completely oblivious to the discrimination between good and evil.'

'Do not doubt my sanity, Maharaja,' said the chief priest. 'It's inglorious to destroy the ageless magnificence of Utkalian art. Again, the God whom we worship in this sacred temple as an embodiment of truth, beauty and goodness is what is precisely reflected in every part of this female dancer. Beauty is not a sin. The eternal bliss which the sculptor breathed into the gesticulations of this female dancer cannot be deemed as a sin. This female statue will help teach a lesson to the obsessed humanity who has turned a blind eye to human existence, the earthly world, and the beauty and charm of human life, in the course of their relentless pursuit of religion, temperance and divinity. To exist is not a crime. This mortal female figure is a concrete reflection of that immortal beauty and unflagging bliss of the Supreme Being who has created this entire universe. The female is not the one who paves the way to hell. The primitive pulses, the ancient allurement of the heart and the heavenly union between the Prakriti and Purusha that bring this beautiful world into existence and fill the creation with infinite grace cannot be a sin. This elegant female figure will spread your glory as much across the world as that lifeless stone image of Lord Lingaraja.'

Yayati Keshari was silently listening to the priest's astute words in rapt attention. A shaft of crimson light from the setting sun glinted on the face of the doe-eyed dancer. Her bewitching eyes seemed to perpetually hold the conflict between the human and God. Natawar stood there like a stone figure, bewildered by his own creation.

'Let's all salute an achievement of truly monumental proportions,' suggested the Maharaja. 'You have made me feel proud, sculptor.'

Yayati Keshari gently pulled a pearl necklace off his neck and slipped it around Natawar's proud neck.

The Ruins

The golden era of the Chaudhury family was about to end at the time of Vishwapati Chaudhury's death. The rich and resourceful Chaudhury Empire, however, was not established during the reign of Vishwapati Chaudhury. Nataraj Chaudhury was the father of Vishwapati Chaudhury. During his reign, company administration was newly introduced in Odisha. At that time, Nataraj was in his youth—clever and efficient. Hence, after gaining the patronage and favour of the white people, holding high offices, he was subsequently able to lay the foundations of the Chaudhury Estate. His entire life was spent fearlessly with absolute support from the company administration. Towards the end of his life, he was able to raise himself to the height of material prosperity, possessing a large estate from Zamindari, including a sky-kissing palace in town, premised with lofty walls and several horses, cars and other movable and immovable properties. But he was too much of a headstrong person—excessively lustful and oppressive. Legends abounded as to how a group of glamorous mistresses waited on either side of the staircase with their plump and prominent breasts and curved eyebrows as he came from the second floor to the court downstairs with slow, lazy steps. He would descend the broad staircase, touching the chin or kissing the beauty spot down the reddish cleavage or the delicate, quivering, rosy lips of these beautiful mistresses.

And being increasingly intoxicated by foreign liquor, he would sometimes end up, settling himself over one of the ladies, standing by his path, with eyes fixed on the ground. With the weight of his bulky body, the woman would find herself squeezed into the wanton wall.

Vishwapati Chaudhury took charge of the estate after Nataraj. He inherited all offensive misdemeanours and weaknesses of his father's character. But his kindness and benevolence in the form of almsgiving were still quite famous among people of these localities. They often cited examples saying King Karna of Satya Yuga and Vishwapati Chaudhury of Kali were made up of the same ingredients. According to one legend that still abounded among the people living in this almost extinct jurisdiction, a poor Brahmin on a hot Vaisakha afternoon appeared at the main entrance to the palace and began chanting the name of Lord Hari. Vishwapati was a staunch follower of Vaishnavism. His passionate heart which had been hardened by materialistic concerns began to overflow with the meandering current of devotion, breaking the bound of worldly benefit and loss, appropriateness and inappropriateness as he heard the name of Lord Hari. Vishwapati sent his men to the poor Brahmin to enquire about his wishes and promised to fulfil them all. But the poor Brahmin said, 'There is no end to human desires; wants are unlimited. Hence, Vishwapati should withdraw his bold promise.' Vishwapati sent his men back to the poor Brahmin saying, 'There may be an end to human wants and desires, but there is no end to God's blessings that eternally shower upon the entire humanity. His kindness is boundless. The poor Brahmin, therefore, can go up to the ultimate limit of his desire. There is no harm also in crossing the limit. Nobody has ever returned disappointed from Vishwapati's door. Vishwapati will keep his promise even if it costs him his entire estate.'

How large would be the limit to this poor Brahmin's unfulfilled desire? Merely a few acres of land!

Vishwapati flashed his most winning smile at the poor Brahmin's solicited demand.

'So shall it be!' said Vishwapati. 'Subarnapur jurisdiction is hereby acceded to the poor Brahmin from this very day.'

The poor Brahmin returned from Vishwapati's palace as Zamindar of Subarnapur jurisdiction. However, nobody had carried out elaborate research to vindicate the truthfulness of this popular legend. But in former times, it was found that a present had regularly been sent to Chaudhury Palace by the Zamindar of Subarnapur on the occasion of the Sunia ceremony every year. Nowadays, it was of course heard from Subarnapur's side that the whole story was a hoax and deliberately perpetrated by the Chaudhury family to soil the reputation of Subarnapur Zamindari. These two postulations, however, ran parallel to each other and had never clashed to date.

During the reign of Vishwapati, the demon of decline had begun to cast long shadows over the Chaudhury family. It had three main reasons. Firstly, Vishwapati's celebrated benevolence in the form of almsgiving had drained much of the wealth and resources, long-preserved in the iron chests and almirahs of the Chaudhury family. Secondly, the rest of the wealth and properties, in accordance with the will, was almost spent on providing sustenance to the offspring of the mistresses, kept by Vishwapati in yesteryears. Thirdly, Vishwapati was extremely stubborn. At the time of his death, he had to sell a vast territory from his jurisdiction to fight a lawsuit only because of his impulsive stubbornness.

Next came Umapati Chaudhury. The pace of decline

quickened during his period. But he did not possess qualities such as benevolence and stubbornness that informed the personality of Vishwapati. He was an idealist and a perpetual dreamer. He had no contact with the world of reality. Three-fourths of the entire Zamindari was sold at auction during Umapati's reign. Chaudhury ancestry continued to run with the remaining capital like a bankrupt merchant's books of account. Had Umapati paid his attention to the remaining portion of wealth and properties, the future of the Chaudhury family would certainly have been different.

Umapati was made of some different stuff. According to his belief, the world including life, wealth and fortune are mere illusions. Like the transient human life, all its losses and benefits are also transient and subject to decay. The only unshakeable truth of life is music. Life has a beginning and an end. But the imaginative, melodious world that is woven out of the tuneful strains is boundless and immune from death and dissolution. Such a world is eternal, inexhaustible, and it is worthwhile to cherish such a beautiful life. He was a great lover of vocal music. A lion's share of his total income from Zamindari was spent to meet the expenditure of the cultivation of vocal music.

Umapati's marriage was finished before Vishwapati's death. His wife Kamalamani often complained about his indifference to work, 'You have lost your vision to see through the reality and failed to prioritise things to our benefit! And if it continues to happen for long, you will see, one day your clerks will replace your position as Zamindars and you will be forced to maintain their accounts for the remaining part of your life. How flourishing a family it was and how it was made to follow a downward trajectory! You should at least think about that, shouldn't you?'

'Perhaps you failed to understand me, Kamal.' said

Umapati. 'Let people live contentedly with their duplicity, falsehood and pretension. But I always prefer a sober and elevated life—full of intensity and excitement. I may be placed in a position either higher or lower than that of humanity. Thus, viewing from any conceivable angle, one may find that I have no connections with the common human life others are destined to live. I do not want to live a mortal life, with its flippancy and awful attention to detail. I want a life that is delicately intertwined with musical notes and intricate melodies. I like my life to slowly merge away into the ocean of eternal stillness, softly floating with its capricious waves, like the thrilling resonance of a tuneful lyre. I do not prefer to attain the hard-earned wisdom of an eccentric or the tart witticisms of an outright fool. I never desired a fragile life.'

'Perhaps you also never tried to understand my position,' Kamalamani retorted. 'Maybe, one day you will be forced to cultivate your vocal music, sitting under the shade of that tree by the roadside. You won't have a roof over your head. And then, you have to quest for that world of fantasy, moving from street to street like a beggar.'

'There is nothing to feel sad about, my dear if such a misfortune befall us,' Umapati replied, softly tapping the reddish cleavage of Kamalamani. 'It could be that you have the pleasure of getting up from the bed of leaves under the benign sky, listening to the notes of raga Bhairavi, played by my veena as the dawn breaks above the eastern horizon. You may find yourself in some melancholic mood, listening to my tunes of sarangi in some lazy afternoon under the desolate shade of some wild tree and the lingering gloom of the evening will drift you into a restful slumber with raga Purabi. And on rainy evenings, as water comes cascading from the roof above your window, your heart may be filled with a pleasing sensation by the soothing tune of raga Malhar.'

Kamalamani remained silent.

Umapati spent his entire life holding such a conviction within his belief system. There was no trouble as long as Vishwapati was alive. He deliberately kept his son away from the world of reality and sufficiently promoted and patronised his cultivation of vocal music. But after his demise, there occurred a sea change in Umapati's familiar world which formerly he had no contact with. There was no money to make instalment payments; the fees of the lawyers were yet to be paid; the final date of a certain lawsuit was due next week and so on. Umapati felt completely baffled at the unexplained urgency of these works and dropped his musical performance for some days. Dust of disesteem began to be deposited over his favourite veena.

Umapati finally agreed to attend the office on repeated requests by Kamalamani. Soon he found himself surrounded by bunches of thick, hard-bound books and records. He was supposed to keep these accounts at the tip of his finger. He needed to closely supervise the works of his clerks and must learn how to handle them well. The works of the estate could not be performed without mastering these skills. Kamalamani gave this valuable advice to Umapati. But after a few days, Umapati stopped attending the court and again busied himself brushing the dust off his favourite musical instruments with his cloth folds.

'How come you return so early from the court?' Kamalamani enquired. 'Don't you know how noxious are those men whom you have placed a great deal of trust in? Do go back again. You should at the least first examine the accounts of the estate for the last ten years. I would rather keep your veena, tanpura and other instruments clean in your stead.'

'Do not compel me any more, Kamal,' Umapati said in an intolerant voice. 'I cannot handle these works. I cannot help granting them pardon who honoured me as their master and food provider for their disparate mild misdemeanours which they resorted to for their modest material benefits. It's futile to search for their mistakes. Why do you view the world with such suspicion and distrust?'

Noticing marks of dissatisfaction on Kamalamani's face, Umapati further explained, 'You again misunderstood me, Kamal. The world, you send me to, is full of ironies, mistrust and hatred. There I must resort to violence and oppression. I hate to persist with such a juiceless world. I rather prefer a world where there is nothing but you, my veena and this melodious, colourful world that resonates with sweet, pleasant notes. Please do not compel me to live in a world devoid of these beauties.'

Right from that day, Kamalamani stopped advising him about Zamindari. She rather preferred to summon the clerks to the palace and supervise the works by herself but never asked Umapati to attend the court again. The clerks also never forgot to grip the opportunity waiting in the wind.

Still, for Umapati, there was no deliverance from this pathetic existence. Suddenly one day he set off on an uncertain, pathless journey to a sequestered land, far from the awful strife of this materialistic world. Kamalamani exploded with grief. But she could not afford to shrivel any longer with grief as the future of the entire family now rested in her person. Hence, accepting her lot, she again began to focus on the works of the Zamindari. But inwardly she nourished the faith that Umapati would return to the palace someday.

And one day Umapati returned to the palace after long seven years of absence. Kamalamani clasped his hands to her breast and said, 'This time I am not going to let you leave so easily!'

Umapati chose to abide in bondage till his last. But during the time of his death, the Chaudhury family was relegated to the status of a common middle-class family.

During the period of Nilamani Chaudhury, the golden moments in the history of the Chaudhury family had become a legend. Nilamani was sensual and extremely concerned with material possession. But despite his being worldly-wise, he had to spend his entire life in poverty and difficulties. One day, suddenly an idea cropped up in his mind that some treasure must be hidden somewhere underneath the foundations of this palace. Nataraj or Vishwapati must have buried pots of gold and coins somewhere under the earth to protect themselves against unforeseen circumstances and problems in the future. And it had been a matter of common occurrence in almost all rich Zamindar families. Who knows, someday he might be able to recover a large quantity of wealth and treasure buried under the earth. And his poverty-stricken, encumbered life would be transformed overnight. Hence, several big pits were dug in the ground, bursting open the foundations in many places. Yet, Nilamani was not able to discover any hidden treasure buried under the ground. Finally, these repeated failures drove him insane. In the course of his treasure hunt, one night, he fell into one big pit and died.

During Rajendra's time, the Chaudhury family had almost become extinct. The two-hundred years old sky-kissing palace, surrounded by lofty walls, gradually fell into ruin, being littered with numerous dark yawning pits.

It appeared as if the worn-out, emaciated skeleton of the Chaudhury family was lying neglected in the graveyard of unending time.

*

The houses on the northern side of the palace had long since been locked. Formerly, some ministerial servants, attendants and gardeners were staying in those abandoned houses. They were not required during the reign of Umapati Chaudhury. Those vestibule-like large houses, therefore, were kept closed for quite a long time. During his destitution, Nilamani was forced to earn his sustenance, by selling off the beams, rafters and internal door pairs of those houses. The houses were fast deteriorating with the walls almost crumbling and levelling to the ground. Standing on the veranda of that two-storey building on the south when one observed that sight under a lack-lustre moon, one might realise that the sunset was far more beautiful than the sunrise. There may be beauty in elevation, but there is vividness in ruination.

Leaning against the railing on the veranda, Rajendra had spent several evenings gazing towards that ruin. The dilapidated walls stood there like wild apparitions in the faint moonlight. The heaps of broken bricks, overgrown with weeds and rank vegetation had created a strange ambience around the palace. But the large wrought brass gate that had been installed during the reign of Nataraj was still intact. During the heydays of the Chaudhury family, two men were specially appointed only to open and close the gate. But nowadays, the gate always remained closed. If one wanted to come inside, one had to pass through the narrow passage formed beside the gate. And on opening the gate, the entire vicinity became perturbed by the odd squeaking sound of its jammed hinges. As if the unremembered, restful past grumbled in protest against the undue intervention on its cool calmness.

The houses on the eastern and the western sides were also found in a similar condition. Yet a few houses among them were almost liveable. But of course, on all other days except the rainy season. After decades of neglect and deterioration, the roofs of the houses began to give way, spraying with showers of rain. As a result of this, the walls were covered in a lush carpet of green moss. Nobody was staying in those abandoned houses for long. But meanwhile, some nameless offspring of Nataraj's mistresses had settled in those damaged houses during the reign of Nilamani. But they had no connections with Rajendra and also never claimed a share in the income from Zamindari. The rest of the houses were populated by bats, pigeons, myna, owls, snakes and many other strange animals and birds. Nobody took the risk of visiting that site after dark. Further, Nilamani Chaudhury, in search of the hidden treasure, had excavated mines after mines on the floors of these houses. The roofs had also been damaged beyond repair. And nobody could say when it might collapse on the top of somebody's head.

Rajendra's area of movement was limited to the long two-storey building on the southern side. These houses were still quite strong as they were being renovated at regular intervals. There were many rooms on the upper floor of this building. Rajendra's drawing room was a big hall in the middle of that floor. On either side of that room were two more rooms which were used by Rajendra and his wife Leela. Other rooms were not required to be utilised by them. The veranda at the front was clean and tidy. Plant saplings such as tuberose, rose, palm, croton and the like were planted along the iron railings. The veranda behind the house looked yet more beautiful. Two big trees, namely champak and almond grew up from the ground and kept the place cool and delightful with its dense leaves and foliage. Rajendra and Leela had spent many moonlit Vaishakha nights on this wonderful veranda. Moonbeams streaming through the mess of leaves and foliage seemed to spread out a silver-dappled carpet on the floor of the veranda.

*

Rajendra had got married before he passed his MA. His mother was still alive at that time. After passing his MA, Rajendra got a lucrative government job, but he was not quite interested in the job.

'It's because of this whimsical attitude that the whole clan perished,' said Leela. 'And you still nourished such a whim in your mind?'

'You may call it a whim, Leela,' said Rajendra. 'But I cannot continue with this job any more.'

It was, however, high time Rajendra got down to serious thoughts about earning some money by himself. It was possible to manage the family somehow with whatever income produced from the ruinous Zamindari. But of course, excluding other pleasures and enjoyment of living. But how long could one survive with such slender means? Living a life of deprivation, sometimes, one might desire to spend lavishly on occasion. In those troubled times, the domestic quarrel between the husband and wife picked up to great heights.

Leela was genuinely perplexed by her husband's moodiness and protested, 'Your attitude is but an outcome of this ruinous Zamindari which you still possessed. And perhaps it is the reason why you grew so wayward over time. But have you ever thought about what will happen when Manu attains his adolescence and Neena's marriage draws closer? Or do you believe that it's not the right time to think about the matter yet?'

'You need not bother about that, Leela,' Rajendra returned, 'as I believe I must be living at that needful hour. It also doesn't make sense to bother about that matter if I won't be alive at that time. In that case, that responsibility is completely yours; hence you should bother about that in my stead.'

Rajendra's exchange of pleasantries aggravated and enraged Leela to a great extent. But he sat there, delightedly enjoying her manner of speaking, punctuated with occasional emotional outbursts.

The broken walls of the palace were appalled at Rajendra's irresponsible, lotus-eating temperament. Rajendra saw before his eyes how the time-honoured ancestry and its revered traditions, which at a point in time commanded the respect of the entire jurisdiction, were gradually merging away each and every moment in the anonymous womb of time like the worn, broken bricks of the towering palace walls. Maybe, during his death, all traces of this great family would be removed from this place, except the mounds of broken bricks, overgrown with weeds and shrubs.

Rajendra silently witnessed everything. Being highly educated, he was sufficiently exposed to all means of earning. Had he strived in this regard, it could perhaps be possible for him to delay this process of ruination. Who knows, maybe a new history and tradition would have emerged from the ashes of the dead past. And it was precisely the thing which Leela wanted Rajendra to understand. But Rajendra's mind was filled with dark thoughts. He was so passionate about the complete obliteration of the past and nourished the dream of absolute demolition in his mind. Let everything be finished and exhausted! Let the great Chaudhury family become absolute paupers overnight! Let the flourished past end up with the ultimate limit of decline! And then, amidst the languor of decline would emerge Nataraj Chaudhury with his glorious, colourful past from the prolonged gloom of that obliterated magnificence. The majestic Chaudhury Palace would be restored to its former glory.

Nobody including Rajendra could check that process of decline as the great family had almost sunk into abysmal degeneration and deterioration. Rajendra sought some solace and comfort in these kinds of thoughts.

But Leela could never penetrate Rajendra's thoughts.

'It stands no reason,' she argued. 'Don't you feel the pangs of shame to spend your life amidst these mounds of broken bricks? The magnificent past which you often boast about is like the book of accounts managed by a bankrupt entrepreneur. Does it make any sense?'

'You seem rather prosaic, Leela,' said Rajendra. 'You lacked that vital spark of imagination in your upturned eyes. May those mounds of broken bricks appear worthless to your juiceless eyes, but for me, they are like the ruinous mausoleums, mentioned down the pages of Roman history. I feel as though I happen to be one of the historical descendants of a certain mighty Roman Emperor, abiding with these broken bricks, rocks and ruinous memories.'

'But can man live by imagination alone, unfettered by the bounds of reality?' Leela retaliated. 'Can dreams sustain life?'

'You are futilely trying to put the blame on me,' Rajendra said, trying to evade her arguments. 'What can I possibly do? Perhaps you do not like my decrepit, dismal existence, backdropped against a glorious, brightly illuminated past. But am I responsible for that, Leela? Nataraj, in his lifetime, was able to raise himself to the farthest limit of glory and prosperity like a rising star. But am I to be blamed if that bright star suddenly merges away in the engulfing darkness of the evening? Why should I feel guilty about myself if that rising star abruptly loses its glowing warmth? The fault rather lies in Nataraj. Had his movement of ascension a bit slower, the pace of decline could have been remarkably delayed.'

Leela still resorted to arguments but to no avail.

'You lacked that sense of fertile imagination in your beautiful eyes,' Rajendra added. 'Hence, you fail to discern the richness and beauty of this wonderful world. You have only noticed the elated aura of the splendid sun as it rises above the eastern horizon, but you cannot see the glowing beauty of the setting sun. You cannot paint a picture exclusively with light. You must require shades to make it look complete.'

Leela remained silent.

Yet at times, their married life ushered in such golden moments when Leela became forgetful of all her sundry complaints about the impoverished life. She began to enjoy her husband's vivid, overactive imagination and his exuberant expression. Reclining on Rajendra's lap on the veranda behind the two-storey building, Leela listened to his words with rapt attention. And Rajendra busied himself narrating the tales and legends of the Chaudhury family which had almost passed onto oblivion: 'On that day when the charming and incredibly shy bride Purnima first stepped into the life of Vishwapati, one of his friends jokingly said that in that inauspicious, dark day of Amavasya, his Purnima, meaning full moon, was but a great lie!

Vishwapati retaliated to this joke by lighting thousands of golden lamps in his palace. The new bride Purnima with timid, downcast eyes proceeded to the bridal bed amidst thousands of dazzlingly bright flames.'

Rajendra abruptly finished his tale, realising the apparent worthlessness of such stories which indeed carried no value in their modest living. Leela had requested Rajendra several times for a gold necklace and a sari. But Rajendra preferred to be silent on every occasion. Irrespective of his idealism and vivid imagination, Rajendra was unable to comply with Leela's modest request. Many destitute people of these localities approached his door on festive occasions in the hope of collecting their baksheesh from the Chaudhury family. And this had become a general trend over the decades.

But nowadays they had to return disappointed from the palace with Rajendra's false assurances. Yet, Rajendra never forgot to cite the story of Purnima for whom thousands of golden lamps were lit to honour her arrival at the palace.

His entire heart became intoxicated with remorse and self-condemnation. Leela said, 'What happened to you again?'

Rajendra leaned into Leela and wrapped his arms tighter around her in a warm embrace. 'Oh, cast them off from your mind, Leela! There may be beauty in vacuity, but there is no pleasure in the beauty that is fraught with silent tears,' said Rajendra as he smoothed away a wisp of hair from Leela's forehead.

'The vividness of your eyes had remarkably reduced,' Leela said humorously. 'You should try pink eyeglasses.'

*

The sun sank below the horizon. The red-hued texture of the setting sun gradually diffused into a pale, hazy complexion. Spreading out its enormous wings, darkness began to swoop down from the wombs of the western sky.

Sprawled untidily in an armchair, lying down on the veranda of the two-storey building, Rajendra fixedly gazed at the bedimmed horizon. The mosses of gloom were gradually spreading across the ruins of fading light.

Leela went on an invitation. One of the distant cousins of Rajendra was a renowned lawyer in the town. Leela was invited to the birthday party of his first child. She was previously reluctant to attend the party as she was scantily clad with gold ornaments except for a pair of slender bangles on the wrists and a pair of earrings in the ears that were designed in the shape of a sunflower. Of course, she possessed a costly gold necklace but that was not generally used by her being out of fashion as of now. Many times, in the past, Leela had insisted to buy a gold necklace for her, or making a new one, exchanging the old on shortage of money. But Rajendra extended no opinion on the matter and preferred to remain silent because that necklace was very old and had great sentimental value for him. Apart from this, Leela had also no fanciful sari to wear on festive occasions. Initially, she, therefore, firmly objected to accepting the invitation to the party. But it was a joint invitation from Ramanath and his wife which she finally could not turn down. Also, Leela must attend the party as a representative of Rajendra because owing to some unexplained reasons, Rajendra did not like to go anywhere on invitation. Hence, it was possible that Ramanath would take it otherwise if none of them attended the birthday party.

'Wow! How beautiful you look, Leela, in your modest attire,' exclaimed Rajendra. 'Like the unadorned, virgin dream of a young poet!'

'I do not want to hear your fanciful stuff at this time,' said Leela. 'I do not like to go there. Yeah, that's it!'

Leela's mind was filled with perfect discontent. She was inwardly greatly displeased with her husband. How insensitive had he grown over the years! He had absolutely no eyes to look through a woman's heart. Many of Uma's female friends would attend the party accepting the invitation. Pearl necklaces would adorn their lovely necks, diamond studded rings would enrich the beauty of their fingers and they would be gorgeously dressed in new, silken crepes or costly georgette. And Leela would feel like a fish out of water amongst them—awkwardly dressed and unornamented. The unadorned, virgin dream of a young poet!

But finally, Leela had to go. Uma had made her swear she would attend the party at any cost. Hence, honouring her request, she ultimately changed her decision. But in fact, she had not gone on an outing from these mounds of broken bricks and rocks for a quite long time. Meanwhile, the moss of melancholy had crept over her colourful mind. So, grasping the opportunity of invitation, her youthful mind became excited with the prospect of rejoicing and festivity. Uma had warmly invited Leela to the party. Leela would remain Leela whether she attended the party in a princess's attire or a pauper's and get the honour due to her person as an invitee. Why should not she go then? Not attending the party would be a downright weakness of the mind!

Leela selected the best sari from her limited stock. All saris, however, looked old and shabby and bore the indelible marks of poverty and deprivation. But each time, she had to comply with Rajendra's choices and wishes. This grey-shaded sari, in Rajendra's view, for example, made Leela look much younger than she was. As she opened the ornament storage box, her attention was first attracted by a gold-plated necklace. It was a large, stunning necklace set with imitation jewels. At first view, it seemed a very costly one, with rare exquisite jewels studded into it. Leela bought this necklace to wear on the occasion of her younger sister Sushama's marriage without the knowledge of Rajendra.

At that time, Sushama had inquired, 'Did you buy this necklace recently, sister? It might cost you a good deal of money, I guess.'

'You too are mistaken, Sushama,' said Leela. 'Is he in a condition to buy me a costly necklace like this? It's a very old one which was kept in his mother's casket under lock and key for a long time. Now I am using it. But the stones studded into it were newly crafted.'

Meanwhile, three years had passed since the necklace was bought but it still looked new because it was locked inside the box since then. No sooner had she reached home from Sushama's marriage ceremony than she could not have complete peace of mind as long as she put it back in the casket under lock and key. She felt as if she had girdled a poisonous snake around her neck.

As Leela's eyes fell upon the necklace today, she wanted to wear it. She slipped the necklace over her neck and glanced at herself in the mirror. Backdropped against her soft rose-petal-like skin, the necklace looked stunningly beautiful. Leela came out of the room wearing it.

*

Seated in his reading room, Rajendra was poring over a book. Leela stealthily hurried into the room and pressed her hands against the pages of the open book. 'What happened, Leela,' Rajendra asked in amazement.

Leela gave a gleeful look to Rajendra and enquired, 'Tell me, how beautiful am I looking?'

'Fantastic,' said Rajendra looking up into her capricious eyes.

'Umm! It didn't go well, try it yet again,' said Leela amusingly, giving a girlish giggle.

Rajendra clutched Leela's hand and questioned, 'Where did you get this necklace from, Leela?'

'Why? Do you think it is rather fortuitous that a daughter-in-law of this family should wear a costly necklace like this?' Leela queried. 'But didn't you say one day that when the new bride Purnima first stepped into this family, thousands of golden lamps were lit in her honour?"

'I'm not bothered about that,' said Rajendra. 'But where did you find this necklace from?"

'I have bought it from the market.'

'Are you poking fun at me, Leela? It must be a costly one.'

Rajendra began to examine the necklace thoroughly with both of his hands.

'A talented person can spot a talent as a goldsmith can truly judge the quality of gold,' said Leela, 'You are not a goldsmith, hence you failed to judge it correctly.'

'What do you mean?' Rajendra gasped in disbelief.

'It's a mere imitation necklace!' Leela explained. 'And the jewels studded into it are but colourful glasses.'

'I won't allow you to wear that thing, Leela,' said Rajendra, pressing both of her hands. 'You should rather go without any adornment.'

'Do not argue,' said Leela. 'I cannot attend the party unornamented.'

'It's not an argument. It's my wish and my order too.'

Leela's eyes suddenly became unnaturally wild with a chilling fierceness.

'Do give orders once you're capable of buying me a genuine necklace like this and on that day, I would be pleased to obey all your orders with utmost sincerity.'

'It's disgraceful to pretend, Leela,' said Rajendra, heaving a long sigh. 'You will be consumed by the pangs of a guilty conscience.'

'A little addition of pretence to truthfulness makes life ever interesting,' Leela replied.

Rajendra's mind became disconcerted with humiliation and indignity.

*

Leela returned after the evening.

The fifth day crescent moon of the bright fortnight was shining merrily against the dotted firmament. Moonlight poured through the dense foliage of the *champak* tree, showering its patchy, silvery beams on the veranda. The evening air became thick with the intoxicating fragrance of *champak* blooms. And the delightful smell of *nageshwar* was inescapably intertwined with it.

Rajendra dejectedly ensconced himself in the armchair. A garland of *champak* flowers interspersed with *nageshwar* blooms was placed in a silver pot on a tea table near him. And a cluster of red oleander blooms was left near the pot. These flowers were a gift from the old gardener which was an age-old tradition prevalent in the family for a long time.

Leela entered the room and sportively sat slouching on the arm of the chair, leaning towards Rajendra. She gently put the necklace off her neck and placed it on a nearby table. Then she breathed a deeply contented sigh. How many times had she lied about this necklace? How much did she resort to playacting only because of it?

'You are quite upset with me, aren't you?' Leela enquired.

Rajendra lifted the garland of champak flowers off the tea table and said, 'Put that necklace off your neck and throw it to the dark. It looks so unattractive to your neck in the light. It's sheer deceitfulness! I cannot bear up against such falsehood and gaudy beautification.'

'I have already put off that necklace, my dear husband,' said Leela. 'What crime have I committed? Those who are deprived, sometimes have to maintain as though they possess everything which life has offered to.'

Rajendra affectionately dragged Leela's body close to his chest and slipped the garland of champak flowers around her neck. Then he tucked some red oleander blooms in her unadorned locks of hair.

A shaft of faint moonlight fell on Leela's glowing face. The *nageshwar* blooms, hanging down the cleavage, between her quivering breasts, softly swayed by her tender breathing. Leela looked like a living goddess—a paragon of eternal beauty—immune to injury and anxiety of death.

Rajendra greeted the quivering *nageshwar* blooms with a passionate kiss and said, 'Sighting you today conjures up pleasant memories of Kamalamani. Would you like to listen to that story, Leela?'

'Yes,' said Leela rather enthusiastically.

'It was an evening in the springtime. Kamalamani insisted Umapati sing a song in Bahar raga.'

'Umapati said, "Let me dress you up, Kamal, in raga Bahar before I begin."

'Kamalamani removed all gold ornaments from her body, clasped a garland of *kurubaka* flowers about her shoulder, wrapped a girdle made of red oleander beads around her slender waist, tucked a fresh sunflower in her locks of hair and donned the anklet of pomegranate buds around her nimble feet.'

Suddenly, Leela's engrossed eyes glinted menacingly in the shimmering moonlight with overwhelming excitement.

'You have turned a blind eye to the world of reality around you,' said Leela, releasing herself from Rajendra's slackening grip. 'You understand nothing. That day, removing her gold ornaments, Kamalamani had worn the garland of *kurubaka* flowers, overcome by a caprice of the mind. She enabled herself to be adorned with *kurubaka* and oleander flowers, struck by a passing fancy and not as an outcome of hardship and penury.'

Rajendra was unprepared for this explosion. He gaped at the enigmatic face of Leela in shocked amazement.

'There is no necessity of boasting about the wealth and status that is gone, blindly holding them in high regard and esteem,' Leela cried out. 'What do you possess today? Don't you feel the pangs of shame in telling me the illustrious story of Kamalamani amidst this penury and ignominy?'

Over the years, Leela had unknowingly developed an invidious jealousy at Kamalamani's lavish living.

She at once removed the garland of *champak* flowers from her neck and angrily hurled it onto the floor.

Rajendra presumably was dozing in his bed. He was rather amazed at Leela's behaviour than being grieved by her apparent erratic demeanour. He was not always able to understand Leela properly.

But sleep eluded Leela's eyes for the whole night. Leaving her bed, she was restlessly pacing up and down on the veranda. She had humiliated and insulted her beloved husband and treated him as a vulgar creature whom he had always showered utmost love, respect and affection merely for a gold necklace.

Penury is not a crime!

Even amidst unglamorous penury, the glory and magnificence of life can be felt in the human pulses. Penury may bedim your outfits, but not your soul!

Rajendra awoke with a start. Warm tears from Leela's eyes were trickling over his sleeping feet.

Pulling off his feet, Rajendra sat on the bed and said, 'You are crying, Leela?'

She buried her face in Rajendra's chest and said in a

tearful voice, 'I was impolite, my husband! I earnestly pray for your pardon. Do forgive my ignorance.'

Leela already gathered the garland of withered champak flowers which she had hurled onto the floor and wore back in her locks of hair. The sweet fragrance of crushed flowers lingered in the air.

'You looked very frail, Leela. I have forgiven you for long,' said Rajendra, pressing his face against her exposed cleavage and breathing the delightful smell of *nageshwar* flowers.

Adima and Shatarupa

It was a clear and sparkling dawn at the beginning of the unfolding of God's Creation. The prehistoric woods and forests had not yet reverberated with the resonance of man's hunger, struggles, union, separation, love and propagation. Adima and Shatarupa, like an initiatory musical prelude to a new song, like the indistinct enumeration of a newly composed poem and like two modest initial lines of an incomplete picture, were set against the backdrop of the endless, sprawling expanses.

Adima used to wander around forests, hills and caves in search of food and generate fire by rubbing stones together. An insatiable appetite and a simmering discontent were his inseparable companions and he was perfectly happy with it.

And by sitting at the edge of the mountain stream, Shatarupa would endlessly weave the phantasmagoria of beauty and charm all day and night. It was her pleasure and delight.

Like any other day, peering at her image reflected on the flowing water, Shatarupa was decorating her locks of hair with leaves, buds and blooms of the early spring. A wild deer, unable to resist the temptation of the tender leaves tucked in her hair, was licking her nape, with a greedy tongue sticking out at her. A sharp thrill of excitement suddenly traversed Shatarupa's brittle body with a strange sensation. It seemed as if the delicate touch of that stranger for which she had been yearning for long had inevitably been etched through that elongated tongue. But who was that stranger waiting for whom every single moment of her had been filled with expectations and pleasurable anticipations? The rustling of the dry leaves in the vicinity at times was creating the illusion of that stranger's footsteps approaching her. She glanced at the desolate forest path in stunned amazement. Adima was returning from the forest with his usual, energetic gait. He had a dead animal slung over his broad shoulders. Seeing Adima, the core of her heart was overwhelmed with an unspeakable, indescribable urge. The girdle of leaves which she had fastened around her waist inadvertently loosened. Heaven knows, why she could not help staring at Adima with wide lustful eyes today.

But Adima proudly flung down the kill and disappeared into the forest. The branches and foliage in the depth of the forest ruffled and rattled restlessly with a seething impatience. Shatarupa breathed a long sigh and again busied herself with decorating her hair, peering at the mirror of water, oblivious to her immediate surroundings.

But it was a new dawn altogether.

The sterile earth, in anticipation of a beautiful and blessed creation, had become expectant like an amorous woman, after ages and aeons of unbounded barrenness. The vast expanses of the wilderness were agitated with a raging thirst for creation. There was no delight in the sounding cataract or the blowing breeze. The rustling foliage of the trees and plants resounded with an intense thirst for creation. The voluptuous wantonness, that informed the curious tongue of that wild deer, was dramatically missing. It was rather burning dreadfully with an all-consuming fire of hunger.

The familiar earth and the dawn seemed different from that of any other day. Shatarupa called out in an ecstatic voice, 'Adima! Adima!'

The empty woods echoed back to her the sound of her voice. Like any previous day, she could not lose herself entirely in weaving the phantasmagoria of beauty and charm by sitting at the edge of the flowing water, with feet dipped in. She disappeared along the desolate path leading to the depth of the impassable forest in search of Adima.

After crossing many a river, mountain, wood and forest, Shatarupa finally discovered Adima near a remote cave. Seated at the entrance of that cave, he was forging a weapon of hunting by rubbing a stone against a rock. The muscles of his upper arms beneath his tanned skin rippled restlessly like the swirling waves of the sea. Shatarupa silently observed his bare body for a moment. It seemed as if the eagerness of her brooding desire danced longingly along his agitated muscles. But Adima did not lift his eyes to steal a glance at Shatarupa's charming face.

Adima's chief delight comprises collecting new weapons of destruction. His heart was never tormented by the thirst for creation.

Shatarupa lifted herself from her perch and sat beside Adima. To attract his attention, she plucked a few blood-red Palash off her tresses and scattered them on the ground. Amid this pretension of inadvertency, she was expecting Adima to fling his weapons of hunting away and adorn her locks of hair back with those glowing blossoms.

Yet not even once did Adima cast a quick look at her. She persisted and moved her hand around his heavy muscles. But he was still unmoved.

Shatarupa went away sulking, her eyes held a menacing glare.

But Adima was yet to grasp the agony of the female heart—her hidden inclinations and unspeakable desires. Therefore, her feigned outrage and angry scowl all went in vain. She quickly came back to him and touched his body. She felt his body to be as tough as a rock. As if he were the unperturbed child of an immovable mountain, carved out of solid stone. She moved closer and crushed her body against him. Yet his muscles did not soften, his pulses did not throb, and neither did his arms encircle her slender waist.

Adima's hunger was only confined to his belly. He had never been tormented by the hunger of the heart. He had only conquered others by force, but never had he been subjected to the orgy of lustful desires. He had burnt others by fire but had never himself been consumed, bit by bit, with libido's smouldering pyre.

He was utterly primitive and devoid of feelings and emotions.

Shatarupa did not lose her patience. Her heart was brimming with the urge for recreation. Every atom of her swayed rhythmically to the pounding call for the union. Shatarupa continued to sit there waiting for Adima.

After a few moments, Adima suddenly threw the incomplete weapons from his hands and rushed into the forest like a wild animal in search of food. Propelled by hunger, Shatarupa followed after him.

After traversing a long distance, Adima suddenly paused under a strange tree. Both Adima and Shatarupa had no idea that each branch of the tree was laden with innumerable luscious and fragrant fruits. Each of the fruits looked indescribably beautiful, attractive, and full of vivid colours. Unable to restrain his greed, Adima picked up a fruit from under the tree. It seemed as if every single tissue of that lovely fruit was replenished with all piled up passions and desires of the world. Adima had so far only enjoyed the profit of destruction but never had he possibly witnessed the variegated beauty of creation. As though all earthly qualities such as indulgence and self-sacrifice, delight and agony, blitheness and misery had permeated the strange fruit. Like a savage, hungry beast, Adima began to nibble at the fruit.

A strangely sharp, bitter-sweet and pungent taste overwhelmed Adima. He shifted his glance and found Shatarupa standing beside him. It seemed to him for a moment as if all beauty and loveliness of the universe had been embodied in her person. There was the youthful invitation of thousand vernal paradises in her flowing locks of hair. Her eyes were filled with the unquenchable thirst for union; her breath was saturated with the fragrant perfume of the spring wind.

Adima had observed her countless times in the past. But today, she was looking completely different—as fresh and appealing as the morning dew. He fondly held the half-eaten fruit closer to her lips and signalled her to eat.

But to his surprise, the same Shatarupa who had been following Adima like a docile, faithful animal through forests, mountains and valleys for a long period, now fled from him as a dismayed deer and withdrew into the farthest refuge in the innermost depths of the forest.

Where was Shatarupa?

The gentle greenness of the forest became stunningly beautiful in an instant reflected with the brilliance of the dark-skinned Shatarupa. The buds and blossoms growing in rich profusion on either side of the forest path reminded Adima of the vibrant flowers adorning her tresses.

Adima followed after her calling, 'Shatarupa! Shatarupa!'

But where was Shatarupa?

Many an impassable mountain, craggy valley and thorny forest path echoed with his passionate call for Shatarupa. But she was nowhere to be found.

Time passed.

Finally, Adima discovered Shatarupa. As usual, peering into the crystalline water of the mountain spring, Shatarupa was weaving her hair into an elegant braid. The swirling wavelets that now enveloped her bare feet created the life song of a perfect union in a spirit of complete self-surrender.

Responding to his call, Shatarupa gave him a cold, fragile look over her shoulder and again engaged herself in dressing her hair, with a look of profound unconcern on her face. Adima was thrilled and excited by the gracefulness of her physical appearance like a hunter elated at the prospect of preying on an antelope. He was suddenly consumed by a reckless, overwhelming desire to lift her in his arms and carry her into some shady, secluded bower in the woods. But he felt completely mesmerised by her bewitching presence. Like a mighty flame of fire, she had dissipated all his unflinching manliness.

'Shatarupa!' Adima called out in a timid, engrossed voice.

Adima came again the next day. He had a cup made of leaves in his hands that was loaded with numerous mellow fruits and exotic blooms. Fresh from a bath, Shatarupa was seated absorbedly on the rocky edge of the stream, her wet ebony hair cascading in loose ringlets like webwork of longing and carnal passion. Adima presented that wonderful gift of fruits and flowers at her feet and called out passionately, 'Shatarupa!'

Shatarupa wished to look up at him. But Adima's muscular, well-built body was suddenly illuminated with the overflowing lights of a thousand splendid stars which blinded her vision. She could not lift her eyes from the stony bed of the stream.

Adima heaved a loud, frustrated sigh and went away.

He came another day and approached Shatarupa carrying a breechcloth made of a strip of deerskin.

'Come on Shatarupa,' said Adima, 'and allow me to dress you up with this delicate and colourful strip of deerskin removing the girdle with tassels of leaves around your waist!'

Shatarupa could say nothing in response. As if words stopped at her lips unsounded. Her face flooded with scarlet shame looking at him. She was absolutely without measure to hide her obtrusive nudity. She quickly crossed her rotund arms over her breasts and protected herself from Adima's impassioned, inviting glance.

Adima's precious gift lay on the ground, unutilised. He gradually disappeared from view along the forest path like the deep, calming breath of the late spring.

He returned the next morning with his hoard of corals, gems and pearls which he had collected from the ocean floor. This time, unable to rein in his emotions, he slipped a string of red corals around Shatarupa's neck. She stood there, with eyes shamefully fixed on the ground. Adima was too amazed to find her bashful body to be so delicate and yet devoid of life. As if she had been carved out of lifeless stones. She even did not respond to his touch.

While he was going away being bitterly disappointed with Shatarupa, she felt like stopping him, holding his hands.

But he had disappeared by the time she stepped on the ground from the golden throne of shame and resentment.

Adima came again the next day.

But this time, there was no invaluable gift in his eager hands. Also, there was no banal entreaty or despairing invitation. He had come today as destitute, being completely deprived of his means and resources. He had possibly no present to bestow save the ardent agony of his wounded heart.

Shatarupa flicked an abstract glance at him and said nothing. Adima did not know what was there in that glance, but the core of his heart began to agitate vigorously beneath his sturdy muscles like a dying animal pierced with poisoned arrows. He could understand nothing as to what was happening right inside his inflamed brain. What thrill and heart-pounding excitement were they that overwhelmed every single particle of his flawless body? What scourge of crippling affliction was that which sought to suspend the motion of the blood in his throbbing veins?

Was it merely a carnal urge for sensual gratification?

Drops of hot tears trickled down his anguished face and fell on his well-developed chest. He was utterly baffled and terrified at the ordeal. Wherefrom tear, like the emergence of mountain spring from the rocky crest, came to his otherwise unfeeling eyes? Why? What for? A maelstrom of unfamiliar emotions crossed his baffled face.

Ah, what a wild, horripilating excitement was that! How painful yet how pleasing! And what mad pursuit to lose oneself in the equivalent other!

Adima's successive generations had of course termed this emotion as love. But in the primitive eyes and nascent feelings of Adima, it appeared to be as heavenly and mysterious as the azure blue sky and the encompassing greenness of the cool, shady forest.

Adima was about to leave but Shatarupa held his hands and pressed him tenderly to her exposed cleavage.

Teardrops pearled at the sides of her brooding face.

Black Eagle Books

www.blackeaglebooks.org
info@blackeaglebooks.org

Black Eagle Books, an independent publisher, was founded
as a nonprofit organization in April, 2019. It is our mission
to connect and engage the Indian diaspora and the world at
large with the best of works of world literature published
on a collaborative platform, with special emphasis on
foregrounding Contemporary Classics and New Writing.